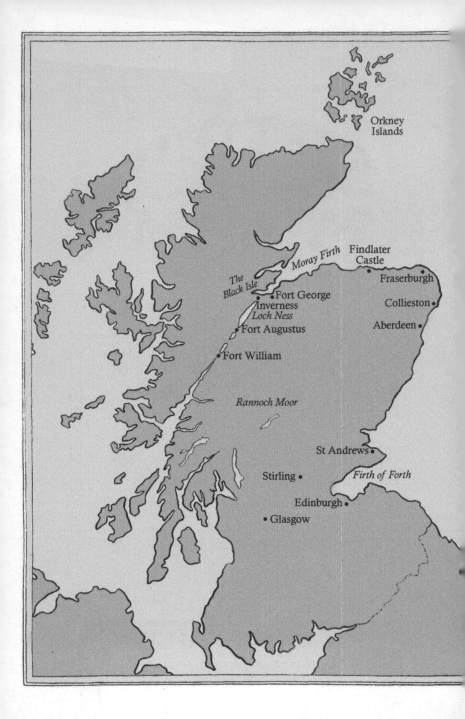

Orkney
Islands

Moray Firth
Findlater
Castle
The
Black Isle
Fraserburgh
Fort George
Inverness
Collieston
Loch Ness
Aberdeen
Fort Augustus

Fort William

Rannoch Moor

St Andrews

Stirling
Firth of Forth

Edinburgh
Glasgow

SILVER STORM

CAROLINE CLOUGH

Kelpies

Kelpies is an imprint of Floris Books

First published in 2016 by Floris Books
© 2016 Caroline Clough

Caroline Clough has asserted her right under the
Copyright, Designs and Patent Act 1988 to be
identified as the Author of this Work

The publisher acknowledges subsidy
from Creative Scotland towards the publication
of this volume

British Library CIP data available
ISBN 978-178250-313-2
Printed in Poland

With love to my wonderful husband, who has listened patiently to many months of deliberations, helped me with the plot and provided me with inspiration. He is my hero!

And love to my children, Charlotte and Rory, and to my big sister Hilary and her family, who have supported me in so many ways.

Thanks to my girlfriends: Laura, Jackie, Sally and Maggie. They kept me going when things got tough!

Many thanks must also go to my my readers, whose constant enthusiasm and interest in my stories have inspired me to write this, the last in the Red Fever *trilogy.*

Finally, thanks to the team at Floris, who have advised and supported me throughout.

1.
A DAZZLING DISTRACTION

Toby jumped up from behind the harbour wall where he had been hiding, catapulted from his doze to being wide-awake in seconds.

"WHAT?" he cried. "They're shooting at us!"

He felt his friend Tash tug at his jacket, pulling him down to where she was squatting.

"Sit down!" she commanded in her strong Russian accent. "Otherwise they soon will be. It's Jamie's fireworks. Look!"

The milky mist of snow had disappeared, leaving a clear sky that was illuminated with a falling shower of gold as the rockets exploded.

BANG! BANG! BANG!

Again the sky was lit up from the other side of the harbour.

"Jamie must be just over there," said Tash, her voice only just audible over the fizz and thud of rockets and the roar of a Catherine wheel.

"Not too close I hope," Toby hissed back. "Otherwise those guards will be on to him!"

Tash didn't respond. All Toby could see of her was the fierce head of her wolf skin pointing upwards as she craned her neck to the sky and gaped at the thousand glittering stars above. "Beautiful. Don't think Snowy likes it though."

Snowy, Tash's huge wolf-dog hybrid, was hiding his head inside Tash's wolf skin, pressing his ears hard to her side.

"It's ok Snowy, I'm here," she soothed.

Toby peeped over the wall just in time to see the two guards disappearing out of view. They had been patrolling the quayside all night, but were now running off in the direction of the rockets.

"Now's our chance," he cried, staggering to his feet, which were numbed to the bone with cold.

Tash stood up and shook herself like a wet dog after a swim, throwing a shower of melted snow from her wolf skin. "Can you see the *Lucky Lady*?" she asked anxiously, picking up her basket.

"Yeah," said Toby. "Moored at the end of the harbour where we left her."

The small harbour at Kirkwall near their peaceful commune was never busy at the best of times, but it looked like hadn't been used at all since the

Corporation's guards had descended on Orkney. Keeping a sharp eye open, Toby led Tash down towards the waterfront. There, bobbing peacefully in the dark waters, was his beloved boat, *Lucky Lady*. Just seeing her brought images to his mind from the last voyage he, his dad and his little sister Sylvie had made when they had sailed from Fort George to the safe haven of Orkney, away from the terror of the fatal red fever that had swept the world. They'd thought all that horror was behind them. They'd started to build a new life here.

Try not to think of the good times. It doesn't help. Just concentrate on getting to Edinburgh. That's going to be hard enough with these winter storms.

Toby hauled up the thick rope that tethered the boat to the quay, and threw it onto the deck. Quickly he lowered himself down the ladder and jumped on board, turning to help Tash descend with her basket.

"You sure the papers are still in there?" he asked nervously. Without them, they would never be able to free the rest of the commune on Orkney.

"Yes, yes, Toby, I'm sure. I checked before we left," Tash replied. "Come on Snowy!"

The big grey wolf-dog stood anxiously whining at the top of the ladder.

"Here boy, jump!"

Snowy paced backwards and forwards before launching himself down on to the deck, landing with a thud.

"Good boy," Tash patted his damp coat.

Toby sprinted for the wheelhouse. He ran his hand along the sun visor where his dad always left the keys, and smiled as they tumbled out. Just as he had done a thousand times before, Toby slotted in the ignition key and turned it over

What if Dad's forgotten to top up the fuel since his last fishing trip?

With trembling fingers he watched the needle on the fuel gauge as the boat sputtered into life. It slowly began to climb – and didn't stop until it had reached F for full.

Good on you, Dad! But how long will it last us?

The door burst open and Tash dashed in. "I've found some fuel stashed in the hold!" she cried. "Your dad was prepared for anything. There's even food and water in the cabin."

"Cheers, Dad!" said Toby, suddenly realising that his dad must have suspected that Orkney might not be as safe as he'd led them to believe. He really had become an expert at survival since the red fever had swept the world all those years ago.

"Ha! Tobes, you should see Snowy – he's dashing round the cabin like a lunatic." There was a smile creasing Tash's tired and drawn face, her white teeth reflecting the fireworks that were still lighting the sky around them. Toby smiled back; Tash was great to have around. She always kept his spirits up when things got tough.

"Let's get this show on the road," said Toby, accustoming himself with the controls. It had been a while since he had sailed the boat.

"What about Jamie?" asked Tash. "Should we wait for him? What if the guards find him?"

It had been Jamie's idea to let off the fireworks to distract the guards. Without this ruse, Toby and Tash wouldn't have stood a chance of escaping with the papers. Toby had been surprised at his offer; Jamie was very bright and bookish but usually left the daring deeds to Toby and Tash.

"I'm sorry Tash, but we can't afford to lose time. Jamie knew what he was risking and we knew this might happen. He'll try and find somewhere to hide out."

As much as he was worried about Jamie, Toby knew they couldn't jeopardise the mission by waiting until the fireworks ran out.

Thank you, Jamie.

Toby kept the throttle low as he carefully manoeuvred the *Lucky Lady* out of the harbour. He knew Tash was upset. "I'm sure he'll have snuck away in time. Plus, he's no threat to the Corporation. The guards won't hurt him even if they do find him." He tried to sound convincing.

"But what if Madame Sima interrogates him like she did you? What if she tortures him until he tells them everything?" cried Tash.

"He won't. He's stronger than he looks," said Toby, but in his heart he knew that Madame Sima would stop at nothing to get answers if they caught Jamie. He'd learnt that the hard way.

There was a long silence between them as the fireworks continued to crack and fuzz in their wake. Down in the cabin, Snowy began to bark.

"I'll go and settle that naughty dog," said Tash resignedly.

Toby nodded. He knew she needed some time to herself.

Funny, I thought Jamie and Tash would never be friends when they first met, and now she's distraught leaving him. I guess we've all been through a lot together.

Toby took a quick glance of the charts his dad had left on the map table beside the controls. He pulled *Orkney and the Northern Isles* towards him to get a better look. He and his dad normally used that map for fishing around the sheltered coves and inlets of the surrounding islands, but Toby had never taken the boat out into these wilder northern seas alone.

I sailed the Lucky Lady *on my own from Fraserburgh to Fort George once – this can't be harder than that, surely?*

But a band of anxiety was tightening across his chest, stifling his breath and sending sharp stabbing pains down his arms.

He clutched the familiar wooden steering wheel tightly in both hands and peered into the darkness. He daren't put the lights on, but fortunately the sky was still lit with gold, blue, red and silver fountains of twinkling lights as the fireworks cascaded down. He edged the boat cautiously forward until they were well clear of the stone harbour walls before pushing the throttle up to full speed. The engines spluttered and spat and the boat roared quickly across the wild waves.

Tash soon appeared at the deckhouse door. "I found a couple of waterproof jackets. Do you want one? It's *so* cold." she said handing Toby a battered old oilskin.

A peace offering.

"Thanks," muttered Toby, peering through the wheelhouse window, and keeping his hands on the wheel that bounced and bucketed under his tight grip.

"Do you think they'll follow us, once they realise *Lady* has gone?"

"I don't know," said Toby uneasily. "You'd better keep watch on deck. Maybe we should've scuppered their boats? But we've got a good start on them. There's a heck of a lot of ocean to search for us if they do give chase."

Tash is right – they're not going to just let us escape that easy. And they've got bigger and faster boats than old Lady.

"They'll probably expect us to go east – either northeast towards Shetland or southeast to the mainland. Let's go west. It'll take us longer but it might confuse them."

Tash nodded and gave Toby's hand, which was still firmly planted on the wheel, a quick squeeze.

Toby grunted back as the boat lurched through the icy waters, the waves slapping nosily against its sides. He stared at the map, looking for a route that might take them westwards away from Kirkwall and round the top of the island. The passage was dotted with small islets – he would have to put on *Lady*'s lights to guide their way around them. He couldn't risk keeping too close to the coastline, then; the Corporation might have lookouts, not to mention the strong currents that could pull small boats onto ragged rocks in shallow water.

"Here, let me steer while you put your jacket on," said Tash.

Toby stood to one side and let her take the wheel, pulling the jacket sleeves over his freezing fingers. "Ok, now just keep your eye open for any rocks. Don't let the boat drag you towards the shore."

"Yes sir!" replied Tash, doffing her wolf head towards him. He knew that Tash didn't like being bossed around, but when it came to sailing she had to bow to his experience.

Tash glanced at Toby as he blew into his hands for warmth. She grinned at him. "It's like old times, is it Tobes?" she said, her English still not perfect despite all the months of lessons they'd sat through in the hall of the fort. "At least we don't have to worry about the dogs any more."

"Think I'd rather face Cerberus and his legion of dogs then that Madame Sima and the Corporation's troops," remarked Toby, remembering how petrified he'd been when the Corporation's guards had stormed the commune in the middle of the night. "We can switch the lights on now – we should be approaching Gairsay soon and we'll need to be able to see to pass through the narrow channel." He took the wheel back from Tash.

"I'll go and keep watch," Tash replied, disappearing out into the bitter cold of the night. But within seconds she was back, eyes wide with fear.

"Toby! I think they are following us! There are lights in the harbour."

Toby snatched up his dad's beloved old telescope and dashed to see for himself. "Just keep her steady and straight," he yelled as he banged open the door and ran onto the deck. He put the telescope to his eye and trained it on the distant harbour. It was scattered with the fluorescent glow of searchlights. As he screwed up his eyes to focus fully through the single lens, he gasped.

There, heading out of the harbour, was what looked like a flotilla of boats led by a large inflatable in which Toby could just make out the shadowy forms of three guards crouched over the helm. One of them was sweeping a large spotlight across the water, whilst the other two appeared to be fumbling with some sort of long metal tube...

They've got a gun!

2.
A DESPERATE DASH

"Kill the lights, Tash!" Toby screamed as he dived back into the wheelhouse and grabbed the wheel from Tash's grip. "They've got a massive RPG gun. If they spot us we've got no chance."

Tash hit the light switches and the boat was pitched into darkness that seemed to swallow them up.

Toby glanced nervously at the compass. "Go and keep watch – shout if they get near," he cried, and Tash dashed outside.

The feeling of dread that now clutched at Toby's stomach reminded him of the time he and his dad – and a very sick Sylvie – had been chased by pirates. His dad had known where to hide because he knew the Buchan coast well: he had navigated the *Lucky Lady* into a secret cave.

But I don't know this coast – I've no idea where to go! Should we try and hide or make a run for it? I wish Dad was here to decide. Surely they won't follow us into Gairsay Sound?

Snow was starting to fall, drifting silently around them and covering the windows with mushy whiteness. Toby flicked on the windscreen wipers, their *dunk, dunk, dunk* beating in time with the racing of his heart as he battled to keep the boat on course. It seemed an age before a snow-smattered Tash staggered back in through the door.

"I think we've lost them Tobes," she announced. "Their lights went the other way. The snow's helping, they won't be able to see anything." She paused, biting her lip. "But what if they realise their mistake and turn around? Can we outrun them, Tobes?"

"We're going to have to try," said Toby through gritted teeth. "I can't sail into a cove in this weather. We'll be smashed on rocks or run aground, then we'll be at their mercy."

He glanced at Tash's ashen face, just visible under the sneering gaze of the wolf mask. Her trembling hands reached out to grab his arm.

"We're going make it, aren't we Tobes?"

Why must I always have to be the strong one?

"Yep!" Toby tried to force a smile but somehow it just ended up as a grimace. "Don't worry, we've got a head start."

"Yes – and it's a good thing, the snow?" Tash tried to smile back at him.

"Absolutely," said Toby. "Now, you go and rest, Tash. We've got a long way to go and we're going to have to take it in turns to steer. I don't know about you but I haven't slept properly in days, thanks to the guards. I'll steer for now but you'll need to be alert when you take over."

"Well if you're sure, Tobes," she replied. "I'm so tired I could sleep for a week."

"Yeah, get your head down for couple of hours," said Toby.

Tash slipped silently out of the wheelhouse, leaving Toby on his own with his thoughts. He prodded his finger on the sprawled map beside him to where he thought they should be by now. They were travelling at about seven knots and had set off from Kirkwall roughly half an hour ago.

We must be approaching Gairsay. Better keep a look out for Holm of Rendall.

Toby remembered navigating around the cluster of rocks while fishing with his dad. He just had to do the same thing again – in a snowstorm, in the dark. He tried not to think about his dad and Sylvie worrying. Or what the Corporation would do to Jamie if they found him. Or whether Madame Sima would punish the islanders once they found out that some of them were missing. No matter how hard he tried, Toby couldn't stop picturing his friends and family cooped up and terrified back on Orkney. He felt a pang of guilt.

I hope Jamie escaped the guards. I hope everyone's ok.

As the *Lucky Lady* stoically struggled through the storm, Toby decided, to keep himself awake, he would recite poems he had learnt at school. That seemed like life in a different universe right now. He recited one of his mum's favourites that she'd taught him years ago: 'The Magic Pebble' by Roger McGough. It made him laugh and reminded him of school, which he'd never thought he would miss.

Toby repeated the poem over and over, concentrating on the words and not on the thought of the pursuing soldiers fixing their sights on the *Lucky Lady* and blasting her out of the sea.

Wish I had a magic pebble right now – I'd magic the Corporation into oblivion! And get Mum back – STOP! Mustn't think like that. It doesn't help.

As the minutes passed slowly by, he had to blink to stop being mesmerised by the constant, oncoming, swirling snow. It wasn't long before his eyelids became heavier and heavier.

Mustn't go to sleep!

But the muggy warmth of the cabin, and that same *dunk, dunk, dunk* of the wipers lulled his senses. Sleep crept over him like a cosy blanket.

CRACK!

Toby was wrenched awake by a loud splintering noise that reverberated through his whole body. The boat shuddered and shook, seeming to stop momentarily before plunging forwards again.

"WHAT was that?" he yelled. He rubbed his tired, gritty eyes with the dirty cuff of his sleeve and stared out into the murky greyness. His glance flickered over the compass. They were no longer heading north-by-northwest towards Gairsay, but due west towards the mainland of Orkney. Toby pulled hard right on the wheel, hoping to correct his course just as Tash dashed into the wheelhouse, shaking the wet snow from her wolf's head.

"Toby! I think we hit something. There was an awful grinding noise."

"I heard it – here, you hold onto the wheel and I'll inspect the hull." Toby went out on the rolling deck and, holding tightly to the rail, flashed his torch down the outer side of the boat. As the boat rose and sank with the pounding waves it was difficult to see, but he could just make out a small crack in the planks barely above the waterline. He flung open the door to the wooden cabin where they slept, and descended the steep steps down to the engine room beneath it. Inside it was noisy, hot and smelly; the air heavy with diesel fumes.

Toby breathed a sigh of relief as he passed the flickering light from his torch over the gloomy space.

Doesn't seem to be any damag— oh no!

A thin silver trickle of water picked up the beam of light and reflected it back. Toby followed the drip down to the floor where an ominous, dark puddle was steadily growing.

We've sprung a leak! Stupid me to fall asleep! How am I going to fix this?

The knot in his stomach was twisting ever tighter, and he could feel a red-hot surge of terror threatening to overwhelm him. Toby took some deep breaths and tried to steady his racing mind. He remembered his dad fixing a hole in the hull once when they had first found the *Lucky Lady*, deserted and forlorn in a harbour near their home in Collieston.

What would Dad do? Ok – first get rid of the water, then stop the leak.

He swept the beam of the torch around the cramped cabin, coming to rest on a metal pump propped up behind the engine. He dragged it over to where the puddle was now a couple of inches deep – and spreading fast across the greasy floor. Splashing back through the cold water, he ran up the steps to fetch a hose from the cabin. Inside, Snowy was lying on Toby's dad's bunk, steadily watching him with his piercing blue eyes.

"It's ok Snowy," said Toby soothingly. He had never quite got used to the huge shaggy beast that shadowed Tash wherever she went.

Clutching the hose, he popped his head round the door of the wheelhouse, battling to keep the look of panic from his face. "We've got a leak! Don't worry – I'm fixing it."

"Ok." Tash's voice trembled and her white knuckles clenched tight on to the wheel.

Toby secured one end of the hose over the edge of the bow and raced back to the engine room with the other end. By the time he got back down the steps, the water had crept up over the crack and closer to the door. He slotted a handle into one side of the pump and the hose onto the other. Then, pushing down hard, he frantically pumped the cold salty water from the floor. Eventually enough water cleared to get to the crack.

Now to seal it up – but with what?

Toby couldn't remember seeing any spare planks or bits of wood lying around the deck, so he sprinted back up into the cabin. He desperately stared around, glancing over Sylvie's wooden bunk bed, remembering how he used to sit with her and make silly hats and waistcoats for Henry, her pet rabbit.

Toby felt a sharp stab of pain as the memories of

his dad and Sylvie flooded back. Was he ever going to see them again?

Wait – Sylvie's bed! Dad made it out of old planks!

He sprang back out into the corridor and guddled around in the toolbox. Coming back with a crowbar and a claw hammer he set about demolishing Sylvie's bed, throwing her duvet and mound of blankets onto a surprised-looking Snowy. He pulled the saggy mattress off next and then, with the hammer, tried to prise the nails out of a plank from the slatted base. The nails seemed determined to cling onto the sturdy wooden frame, and would not budge, no matter how hard Toby pulled.

Only one thing for it.

He picked up the crowbar and tried to lever the edge of the plank away.

"Come ON!" Toby cried through gritted teeth. "NOW!"

CRACK!

With a loud splintering noise the plank broke free, sending Toby reeling backwards into the table in the centre of the cabin.

"YES!" he almost laughed, picking up the shattered piece of wood. All he had to do was nail it into place, but with the boat rolling and pitching like a bucking horse, this would be hard.

Clutching the hammer, plank and some nails from the toolbox, Toby leapt back down into the engine room with a splash. The inky water was now ankle-deep and lapping at the foot of the steps. Toby grasped the pump handle and yanked it up and down to clear the puddle again.

As he sweated over the pump, the water level began to fall sluggishly, leaving the dripping crack in the hull exposed once more. Toby stopped to draw his breath and wiped the beads of sweat from his brow with the back of his grubby hand.

He climbed over to the wooden struts and wedged himself awkwardly between them and the side of the boat. Gripping the torch in his mouth to throw a wavering beam onto the crack, Toby pressed the plank onto the hull and hammered the first nail into a crosspiece.

Suddenly the boat lurched violently to the port side, tossing Toby from his perch to land on all fours in the sticky puddle below. The nails scattered under his palms in the greasy darkness.

No, no, no, no.

Frantically he groped around in the murky morass, his teeth aching from holding the torch, and his fingers and toes numb with the cold. After what seemed like hours he managed to find the other three nails, which were now tacky with wet sludge. He climbed back into the gap between the struts, rode the constant pitching and plunging of the boat, and hammered them slowly in.

Finally he climbed down and surveyed his handiwork. He sighed deeply with relief; only a tiny dribble was now trickling down the wood.

Well, it wouldn't impress Dad, but it'll do for now.

He gave the pump a couple of quick blasts on the lever, and then trailed back up the steps, shaking his head slowly.

3.
SILVER SEAS

"Hi Tobes," said Tash, as he wearily traipsed into the wheelhouse. "Got it fixed?"

"Yep – just hope it holds until we reach somewhere safe where we can repair it properly."

"Why don't you go and have a rest?" said Tash. "Looks like you need it after that. I can cope here for a couple of hours. Honest." She attempted a smile from under her wolf skin. "Snowy can keep me company."

"Ok, if you're sure. I am *totally* knackered. If I'd been more alert we wouldn't have hit those rocks." Toby struggled to meet Tash's gaze as he closed the wheelhouse door.

Can't believe I gave Tash a hard time about staying alert and then fell asleep myself!

Toby went back to the wheelhouse, relieved that he wouldn't have to share the bunk bed with Snowy. The huge rangy wolf-dog was curled up in the nest of duvets and blankets Toby had thrown off Sylvie's bed.

"Hup!" he cried. "Come on – your mum wants you."

Snowy opened one eye and stared balefully at Toby, then dignifiedly disentangled himself from the bedclothes, stood up and stretched. Toby opened the door, grabbed firm hold of Snowy's collar and braced himself again for the snow-blown night.

Snowy greeted Tash with great enthusiasm, jumping up and licking her tired, drawn face. She laughed and patted his shaggy head, visibly strengthened by her pet's affection.

Animals always love Tash – wish I could have that bond with them. It must be great.

Toby made his way back to the cabin and threw himself onto the mound of duvets. He drew them closely under his chin and, closing his eyes, fell into a restless slumber.

His troubled sleep took him back to the fort community on Orkney. The panic and terror he had felt when, out of the night sky, hundreds of the Corporation's soldiers descended on ropes from helicopters like inky black spiders.

The masked invaders isolated the living quarters of the fort, then drove the petrified islanders inside and barricaded them in to make one large prison cell.

Toby juddered in his sleep as he re-lived each moment: Crouching at the back of the room with the rest of the islanders, his dad and Jamie either side of him; their rising horror at the arrival of the Corporation's board; the cold face of their formidable chief, who called herself Madame Sima, striding in and taking charge. Toby could hear her voice as if she was in the cabin with him.

"...as survivors of the red fever, you must all possess genetic immunity to the terrible disease. The Corporation is developing a vaccine and it is your obligation as survivors to cooperate with our testing methods in order to protect those people in parts of the world that the red fever has yet to reach. It is our duty to rebuild what's left of the human race by whatever means possible."

Without further discussion, her guards marched Dr and Professor Pettifer – George and his sick wife Layla – through the cell doors and locked the rest of them in. What followed were more interrogations of the other elders of the community: Toby's dad, Jamie's mum and their friend Murdo. And then, inexplicably, Toby himself was dragged before Madame Sima.

There was something inherently evil about her: the way she looked like she'd just stepped out of the pages of a glossy magazine, the way she looked at Toby with cold, dead eyes as she interrogated him.

"Why me?" In his sleep, Toby relived the terror he had felt that day.

But Madame Sima never explained any of their 'testing methods'. As the image of her leaning threateningly over him, screaming with rage, seared itself onto his mind, he woke with a shuddering jolt.

Ugh! That was totally freaky! I could almost smell her breath! I hope she hasn't punished the rest of the islanders for our escape. We've got to get to Edinburgh and back to them fast!

A shaft of sunlight stabbed through one of the small round portholes in the cabin, warming his toes. Groggily he threw back the sweaty bedclothes.

How long have I been asleep? Hope Tash is ok – think I would've noticed if Lady *had gotten into trouble.*

He stumbled out of the cabin to be welcomed by a sharp sunlit morning. Toby squinted out to sea, scanning the horizon for signs of pursuing boats. All around him the water looked like molten silver in the glinting sun. The night's strong winds had dropped, but a bitter breeze still blew in gusts across the deck.

"Hello sleepyhead," said Tash as he staggered into the wheelhouse. Toby could see from her face that Tash was on her last legs. Dark shadows smudged under her eyes and she couldn't stop yawning.

"Go and get some sleep, you look exhausted," he said, moving to take over the steering. "Have you spotted any other boats?"

"No, none at all – but you must see something. Look out of the port side," she replied, handing him a pair of binoculars. "They're amazing!"

"What am I looking for?" asked Toby as he trained the binoculars through the windscreen out across the ocean. "OH! What are those?" He gasped as, about a hundred metres away to the port side, he spied what looked like three large black sails cruising through the silver seas.

"Orcas!" cried Tash. "Aren't they beautiful? They've been swimming alongside us for miles. Wait until you see them surface – they're enormous." Just then one of the three dorsal fins began to rise upwards to reveal a huge black-and-white body surging majestically out of the sea. The whale blew a massive spray of water into the air before plunging back into the frothing waves.

"You're not kidding!" exclaimed Toby, as the foaming wash from the displaced water hit the *Lucky Lady* broadside on, throwing him and Tash sideways. "What kind of whale did you say it was?"

"Orcas, silly, or killer whales," she replied. Tash was the animal expert. She had learnt so much from her father who had been a wildlife ranger and animal trainer.

"Killer whales? Aren't they dangerous? They're big enough to smash *Lady* up with one flick of their tails!"

"No, Toby, trust me. They aren't dangerous in the wild. Just curious. But my father told me that many used to be kept in captivity, in tiny pools. Some of them killed their trainers out of frustration."

"So they *are* dangerous then?"

"*You'd* be dangerous if you were locked in a tiny cell for years," said Tash.

Toby thought of the islanders they'd left behind, huddled together in cramped conditions while the Corporation took them away for inhumane testing, one by one. "I suppose we did a pretty dangerous thing trying to get away from captivity on Orkney."

"Exactly." Tash took a deep breath as they watched the gigantic creatures swimming effortlessly alongside *Lady*, their distinct white markings flashing through the water. "Do you think Dr Pettifer was right to send us to Edinburgh? What if we can't find their colleague there? And what if he can't help us?"

"Well, it's the only plan we've got. Better than being tortured anyway." Toby's mind was racing with all these questions too, so he turned his mind to something solid. "Right, where are we on the map?"

Tash leant over and stubbed her finger on a wide expanse of blue. "I think we're somewhere in here – the Pentland Firth. I've been trying to keep to the coastline to watch for landmarks. Think we've passed the Old Man of Hoy – that pillar thing that sticks out into the sea. Didn't your dad take you there once to go climbing?"

"No," said Toby sadly. "He promised he would, but he was always too busy running the island with George Pettifer. And now he's got Katie, well... he doesn't have that much time for me any more."

"You're not jealous about Jamie's mum are you, Tobes?" asked Tash.

Toby felt his face reddening. He wished he hadn't said anything. "No, just..."

"Your father, he works hard for the islanders, putting up the wind turbine and fixing the radio mast. That's why he's so respected. He doesn't mean to neglect you..."

"No, I know..." Now he *really* wished he hadn't said anything; it made him sound so selfish. Sylvie never complained even though she had less time with their dad too.

Tash gave him a quick hug. "He will be so proud of you when we return from Edinburgh with the professor. And after all, if it hadn't been for you, we would never have found out that he was still alive. You gave the Pettifers hope again!"

Toby sighed, and nodded. He had withstood Madame Sima's interrogation and told her nothing, but she had told Toby a name – MacDuff – a name the Pettifers knew well. They had thought MacDuff was dead, but Sima had let it slip that MacDuff had escaped the Corporation's evil clutches and was alive somewhere in Scotland. Only George Pettifer guessed where he might be hiding.

"You've been so brave, Toby," Tash told him, patting on the shoulder. She grabbed Snowy and left the cabin.

"Right, man up Toby," he said out loud, trying not to feel sorry for himself. He glanced at the map. If Tash was right they had to keep a southeasterly course to take them round Duncansby Head and into the North Sea. Then they would follow the mainland coast south, down past the Moray Firth, which led inland to Inverness, then eastwards to Fraserburgh. After Fraserburgh, it was south all the way to Edinburgh.

"That's not so difficult is it?" he asked himself. But the sight of those whales surfacing to the port side of the boat made him uneasy. What if they came closer – would the *Lucky Lady* capsize? And what if the Corporation was hiding in some cove somewhere along their route?

Don't think of that… just concentrate on the task. Get to Edinburgh. Find MacDuff.

4.
PRECIOUS PAPERS

The hours seemed to tick slowly by as Toby sailed the *Lucky Lady* on and on through the glittering seas. He'd found his dad's favourite Aviator sunglasses and put them on, smiling occasionally at his reflection in the cabin window.

Looking good!

His eyes flickered over the speedometer, which showed that they were still travelling at about ten knots. By his calculation, they had almost one hundred miles to go, meaning that, if they kept this speed up, they would be arriving about seven o'clock in the evening, long after it got dark.

Tash appeared eventually, carrying a tray of hot tea, some biscuits, dried fruit and nuts, and a jar of peanut butter into which Toby simply dipped his fingers.

"I found a tin of corned beef for Snowy's tea, too. Thank goodness your dad left the boat stocked up!"

"Yeah," replied Toby. "I suppose after all we've been through he never lost that sense of having to be prepared for the worst."

"Look Tobes," exclaimed Tash, "the orcas are still with us! There's a baby one – isn't it sweet?"

Toby swung his focus round to watch the whales, seeing a dolphin-sized black-and-white object gliding through the water close to the others.

"Sweet?" He laughed. "I doubt whether you'd think it sweet if you fell in near it."

"Don't tease, Tobes, you know I can't swim." Tash flashed a smile at him, and then a frown creased her brow. "What are those marks on your wrists?"

Toby glanced down at the mottled bruises on his arms. "Oh, must've been from when the guards dragged me in front of Madame Sima," he told her.

"What did she say?"

"Oh, horrible threats – she'd do this and that to the others if I didn't persuade Dr Pettifer to cooperate. Dunno why she picked on me though."

"Hmm. Well, maybe because people listen to you and your dad in the community," said Tash thoughtfully. "And if what your dad said was true, if they'd been listening in to our radio conversations with the other survivors on the mainland for weeks before they invaded. Then maybe she'd heard about your exploits battling the General, and the dogs. You're quite a celebrity in the community."

"Yeah, and look where my little rebellion got me!" Toby ruefully rubbed the top of his head where a soldier had cuffed him hard.

"They must've heard us talking about the Pettifers on the radio before they invaded – how else could they have known the scientists were on Orkney? I don't know why the Corporation is so interested in them. But they obviously thought that the *other* professor was with the Pettifers. MacDuff I mean."

"Yeah, poor George and Layla," sighed Toby. "They were terrified."

"Do you know what's wrong with Layla?" asked Tash, snuggling up on the captain's chair. "I mean, why she doesn't talk?"

"Yeah, sort of. Katie thinks that she's suffering from some sort of post-traumatic stress disorder," said Toby.

Jamie's mum, Dr Katie McTavish, kept a close eye on everyone's health on the island.

"Still," Toby continued, "it got Layla out of being interrogated by Madame Sima." He shuddered at the memory of his own interrogation.

"True," Tash shuddered. "I wonder what happened to her that made her stop talking. And why Madame Sima was so obsessed with finding them and this MacDuff guy."

"Well, we're gonna beat her to him!" said Toby, trying to sound enthusiastic.

"But what if she tortures information out of them and the Corporation follow us to Edinburgh?"

"They won't give anything away," said Toby. "Plus, George made it pretty clear he thought MacDuff was dead until Sima started demanding to see him."

"So… if George thought he was dead, how did they know he'd be in Edinburgh when they found out he was alive?" mused Tash.

"Back-up plan." Toby shrugged his shoulders. "George told me before they dragged him away for more questioning. Apparently they always planned to rendezvous in Edinburgh if they got separated after escaping from the Corporation, only they never went to find MacDuff because they thought he was dead until now. George said Layla would show me where to find the papers and gave me *this*." He held up a necklace with a tiny amulet in the shape of a horse.

"How is this horse supposed to help us?" said Tash.

"Only one way to find out," said Toby.

Tash sighed. "I do hope Jamie is ok. I worry about him."

"I wouldn't worry about him," said Toby, trying to sound convincing. "He always lands on his feet. He's probably curled up in someone's old bed with a hot dinner inside him."

I hope. If the Corporation has got him to talk, we could be in big trouble.

Toby kept scanning the coastline for recognisable landmarks. Inland there was the Black Isle with its purple hills dusted with snow, sheltering the inlet to Inverness, on whose banks stood Fort George. He recalled how the once-mighty fort had been the scene of a bloody battle between the General's raiders and a massive pack of dogs made ferocious and intelligent by the red fever. Further on was Findlater Castle, jutting into the sea, its empty windows staring sullenly out at him. That was where he had first spotted the dogs that had been tracking him. It all seemed such a long time ago.

About lunchtime they sailed past the familiar town of Fraserburgh, followed closely by the high walls of Peterhead harbour. They hid within them a tangled mess of boats, large and small, desolate and deserted, left where winter storms had thrown them. Toby remembered the time he'd had to hide *Lady* there from the marauding pirates. He wondered when he had been more scared: then or now?

Tash came and stood silently next to him, watching the grey clouds as they gathered on the horizon. "Looks like a brewing storm is coming," she commented.

"You mean a storm is brewing!" said Toby, smiling.

"Yeah," mused Tash. "Is 'storm in a teacup' the same thing?"

"Ha! No – that's something completely different. Here take the wheel, I'm just going to go and put on another jumper," he said. "It's flipping freezing."

Toby left the wheelhouse and went round to the deckhouse, heaving at the clumsy levers on the heavy steel door that kept it watertight in a storm. Inside the cabin he spotted Tash's basket and couldn't help himself taking a peek – just to check the Pettifers' papers were still there.

Getting neurotic now, he told himself as he opened the lid. A sheaf of yellowing parchment lay on the top. He picked it up, puzzled. Was this really what all the fuss was about? The papers were covered with chemical equations and squiggles; he couldn't understand any of it. Whatever it meant, it was very important. George's words rang in his ears:

"Layla will show you where to find the papers.
You mustn't let them fall into the hands of the
Corporation! If they develop a vaccine first they'll

*vaccinate only their own people and use the red
fever to take over everything; they'll hold nations to
ransom. Do you hear me? They're only interested in
grabbing power, not in helping mankind AT ALL!"*

Toby's hands shook a little as he carefully placed
the papers in an old brown envelope and slid it back
in Tash's basket. The envelope contained a crumpled,
water-stained letter on which was a heading: THE
UNIVERSITY OF EDINBURGH. This was their
only clue as to the whereabouts of George and Layla's
colleague. How desperate must the Pettifers have been
to entrust Toby with such a mission?

But Toby knew the answer to that. They were *all*
desperate. They knew what the Corporation could do
if they got their hands on a vaccine; they'd already
seen what Madame Sima was prepared to do to the
islanders to get her way. Toby shook himself out of his
reverie and, snatching a jumper from a bunk, returned
to the wheelhouse.

"Oh, I thought you'd been washed over the board,"
Tash said, seeing Toby pulling on his jumper.

"Ha, very funny," replied Toby. "I was just checking
the papers were still safe."

"Tell me Tobes, how did y'know where to find
them? How did they keep them hidden from the
Corporation's guards?" They'd been in such a mad
panic to escape Orkney, Toby hadn't time to discuss
all the details of the mission with Tash.

"Well, when I showed Layla the horse amulet,
something must have clicked in her mind 'cos she gave
me a postcard."

"What of?" asked Tash.

"It was of the Italian Chapel. It was ancient and sort of faded but I could just make out the fancy door and corrugated iron roof. Dad took me and Sylvie and Jamie there for a picnic once. It's really cool; built by the Italian prisoners of war detained on Orkney during the Second World War. They made it look like the Sistine Chapel in the Vatican in Rome, and it's all made out of concrete!"

"Wow! Were the papers hidden there?"

"Well, the chapel is quite a walk away from the fort, across the Churchill Barriers, and I didn't think that George would've taken Layla that far, with her not being well and that. So before I tried escaping and going all that way, I decided to check whether they were somewhere inside the fort that was linked to the chapel. I remembered hearing some of the elders talking about an old Bible that used to be kept at the chapel. They had brought it back to the fort to keep it safe in Dad's office. And that turned out to be right: the research and the envelope were interleaved between the Bible pages."

"That's SO clever," said Tash, smiling at him.

"I get the feeling the Pettifers and MacDuff must have been very important scientists back before the red fever hit. So I guess if anyone's going to be able to outsmart Madame Sima, it's them."

"It's good that they trusted you," said Tash.

"Well, they had to. It's not like they could slip off unnoticed when Sima was watching them so closely. Plus, we were the only ones small enough to escape through the old sewer pipes. And I wouldn't have been able to do it if I hadn't had you and Jamie there too!"

"You don't think that this is a shot-long going to Edinburgh?"

"You mean a long shot," Toby corrected her. "Yeah, I do. But what choice do we have?"

"Umm, I worry this will be a goose's wild chase and we'll be miles from our families that need us so."

Toby didn't correct her this time but instead shrugged and tried not to look too concerned. Just then, something caught his eye on the dashboard.

"Oh no!" he cried. "We're nearly out of fuel!" He raced out of the wheelhouse to the hold where he picked up the fuel cans and shook them. They were all empty.

We must've been going a lot faster than I thought! Where on earth are we going to find fuel around here?

5.
LONELY LIGHTHOUSE

Toby dashed back to the wheelhouse and frantically rummaged through the maps. "We're nearly level with Collieston, I think," he said. "Maybe we should go to our old lighthouse; Dad had a secret fuel store there. We can patch up the boat there too."

"The lighthouse where you used to live? I'd like to see it! Sounds like it was a cool place," said Tash.

"It was. The view from the lamp room's amazing. Dad got the mirrors and light working, but we never used them in case it attracted the pirates. I hope *they* aren't still around."

"They've probably picked the place clean and moved on to somewhere new," said Tash, hopefully. Both of them knew that the *Lucky Lady* would be no match for a high-powered inflatable full of guns and rockets.

Don't think about it! Concentrate on getting Lady *to the lighthouse.*

As Toby swung the boat west, the black forbidding cliffs of the coast rolled into view. He checked the map; they looked like the Bullers of Buchan, where his dad had towed *Lady* into a cave to hide from the pirates. Toby knew where to go now; it wasn't far. But would it be safe?

The small wooden jetty came into view. Toby eased up the throttle to lower the engine to a soft purr, and slowly edged the boat to butt up against the landing stage. Tash picked up the rough rope from the deck, leapt out nimbly, and secured the boat to a post.

Toby cut the engine, transferred the Pettifers' research to his rucksack and joined her. His legs felt wobbly as he got used to the feel of solid ground that didn't buck and rear with the movement of the waves. In front of them stood the solitary lighthouse, jutting out on the promontory beside the sprawling seaside village. High walls topped with barbed wire surrounded its whitewashed tower. His family had thought that they were safe here from the race of ferocious, intelligent dogs that had swarmed the country. They had been wrong.

"Keep a look out for any dogs," commanded Toby, determined not to be caught unawares ever again.

"You don't think they'd come back here, do you?" asked Tash, trotting alongside him.

"You never know. Cerberus may have returned to his old hunting ground. We don't know what happened after the battle between the dogs and the wolves at Stirling Castle."

As Toby strode towards his old home with its heavy double gates that creaked and groaned in the breeze, he had mixed feelings. There were happy recollections from when his mum had still been alive, before the dogs had made it impossible to travel across land.

But a stab of pain pierced his heart as he recalled his mum's accident and the guilt that he'd suffered afterwards, knowing his dad blamed him for her death.

Then there had been the months following, when Sylvie had gotten so ill. Toby and his dad could only watch as she faded away in front of them, racked with pain and fever. If it hadn't been for Toby rescuing Jamie and his mum from the dogs in Aberdeen, Sylvie might not be here now...

Sylvie! Please God, don't let that evil Madame Sima hurt a hair on her head!

Inside the lighthouse compound, the yard still showed signs of his dad's hasty departure: empty, soggy cardboard boxes littered the ground; pieces of discarded wrappers blew like confetti in the wind; weeds had sprouted between the cobbles, giving the place a desolate, unkempt look. Then there was the shed that Jamie had kept his dog Belle in, and further on was the shed that Monty, Toby's collie dog, had escaped through. That was a twist of fate that cost Toby's mum her life. He shook his head.

Don't think of the past. It's too painful.

Sensing his pain, Tash placed a hand gently on his arm and squeezed it.

"It's ok, Tobes."

He mounted the steps that his dad had built up to the lighthouse. They had been attached to a pulley system so that they could be raised from the inside to make break-ins impossible, but the family's quick exit meant they'd had to leave it open.

On the ground floor there was an eerie silence. All around them were signs that someone or something had been ransacking the place, looking for something. Saucepans, broken cups and plates were strewn about the floor of the little kitchen, and Sylvie's old day bed, an ancient battered sofa, had been ripped to pieces, its white fluffy innards spewed across the planked floor.

"Looks like the dogs have been here at some point," Toby croaked, scuffing an empty tin can with his toe.

"Yeah, but doesn't look like it was recently," said Tash, picking up a half-eaten rubber ball.

"Better check to make sure there's nothing worth saving," said Toby, pulling open a cupboard where they used to store dried food and tins. "Nope, think they've had anything edible."

He slowly mounted the steep stone steps that coiled around the inner wall of the lighthouse, pausing at the open door to his dad's old bedroom. Everything inside had been torn into shreds and scattered across the floor. A picture of a clown, scribbled by Sylvie in yellow and orange crayons, swung lopsidedly from a beam where it had been pinned. He peeled it off the wall, pocketed it and went up another floor to his old room. Again he surveyed the damage, stopping to pick up the tattered remains of his favourite *Star Wars* t-shirt. His mum had given it to him for Christmas a long time ago.

Tash appeared in the doorway. "Hadn't we better get going? I don't like it here. Feels spooky."

"Just one last look at the lamp room," Toby replied. It had been his favourite place to hide from the constant chores and demands that had dominated their battle for survival. Here, he used to imagine he was a balloon, floating through the sunlit sky over the blue sea with only the squawking gulls for company. But today the huge windows showed a gloomy, glowering sky full of dark clouds. It seemed to mirror his mood as he felt an oppressive wave of sadness wash over him.

Why is life so hard? I wish Dad was here. I'm so tired.

Toby felt tears pricking behind his eyes, and a sob tore from his chest. He coughed to suppress it.

Man up! What would Mum say if she saw you feeling sorry for yourself? Chin up! We've got to keep going!

He wiped his moist face with the back of his grubby jacket sleeve and sped down the stairs.

"Let's go!" he cried as he landed back in the kitchen with a thud, surprising Tash, who was busy opening drawers and cupboards in her quest to find anything useful to take with them.

"Where shall we look for fuel?"

"It's stashed in an old truck in the shed," said Toby.

It took the two of them several minutes of straining and shoving to get the doors to the dilapidated shed open. Inside was a rusty old Land Rover, looking like a dinosaur waiting to come back to life. Toby wrenched the door open and leapt in. He threw back a musty blanket to reveal two jerry cans hidden in the boot.

"Yes! We're in luck. And they're full. Here, give us a hand, Tash."

"Thank the goodness for that!" exclaimed Tash, helping Toby to drag them out. Trailing a can each, they slowly made their way back down the path to the *Lucky Lady*. The light was beginning to fade.

"We've lost time, and it looks like a storm is coming," said Toby. He pointed at the clouds that were lowering in the sky, threatening the waves with a lashing downpour sometime soon. "There's no time to properly fix the crack in the hull. I'll get *Lady* going. You fill up the fuel tank," he shouted over the rising wind.

Tash nodded and made for the deckhouse, hauling a jerry can behind her, while Toby stepped into the wheelhouse and turned over the ignition. As the engine coughed into life, he swung the boat away from the shore, flipping on the lights as the dark sea danced in front of him. He was determined to get to Edinburgh that night. There was no more time to lose.

6.
A RUINED CITY

As night descended, the wind started to rip and howl through the boat, tossing it like a piece of flotsam on the rolling waves. While Toby battled to stay on course, Tash dashed into the wheelhouse, bringing with her a stinking waft of diesel. She looked like a drowned rat with her long black hair plastered to her head.

"It's getting rough out there," she gasped, pulling strands of hair from her face and shaking the water from her wolf skin. "Do you think we should rest up somewhere safe? We could stop at Aberdeen?"

"No," Toby yelled above the wailing wind and the roar of crashing waves. "*Lady* will be fine! Think of everyone back on Orkney – we can't afford to waste any more time." He glanced at Tash's white face and could see she was terrified. He had to keep her busy. "Can you check the hatches are all bolted tight? And put your safety line on, I don't want you getting washed overboard. Can you manage?"

"I'll be fine," she cried in a strangled voice.

That was one of the things Toby liked about Tash; she could put on a brave face when things weren't going well. He didn't like sending her out into the driving rain and freezing wash that splashed overboard, but they both knew he was better at steering the boat as it pitched and plunged through the storm. One second they'd be surging down the bottom of a wave with nothing but deep dark water surrounding them, then the next they'd be perched on the crest of the high, rolling surf, hanging in mid-air before plummeting back downwards again.

The storm raged around them for what seemed like days, when in fact it was only a few hours. As the wind started to fall to a sigh and the boat stopped rocking, Tash managed a smile.

"See," she said. "Told you it wouldn't last."

Toby smiled back. "Yeah, just got to find Edinburgh now, and somewhere to park." He glanced at his maps and reckoned that they must be nearing the entrance to the Firth of Forth. Soon they would be sailing towards the towering road bridges and the famous rust-red railway bridge that spanned the mouth of the firth. Not that they'd be able to see them now that nothing was ever lit up at night. He steered the small boat closer to the shore and slowed the engine to a quiet putter.

"Here, you steer while I look out for a safe place to moor," said Toby, stepping out into the freezing air. His breath blew plumes of white into the darkness as he stood on the deck and peered out, watching for familiar shapes to appear out of the darkness. As they sailed closer and closer to the once-buzzing port of Leith beside Edinburgh, he could make out the huge shadowy form of an elegant yacht, its ripped and weather-worn bunting flapping and cracking in the breeze.

"Cor," he said, "look at that. Makes *Lady* look a bit tatty."

"What is it?" asked Tash, peering out of the window.

"That's the *Royal Yacht Britannia*. My dad brought me here to see it when Sylvie was a little baby, back before the red fever when life was normal. We went round all the royal apartments. There was gold furniture and four-poster beds – it was *so* cool. Whoa! Stop the engine – I can see a space for us."

Tash cut the engine and the boat quietly bobbed forwards. "Steer to the right, about thirty degrees! That's it, a little more, yep, nearly there…"

With one huge effort Toby grabbed the thick rope and launched himself up and to the fore, where he could just make out the shadowy form of a quayside. He landed with a thump, skidding wildly across the glittering frost on the concrete, and then quickly recovered his balance. He wound the rope around the nearest bollard and brought the *Lucky Lady* to a gentle bump against the rubber tyres lining the harbour walls. Warming up his hands, Toby jumped back on board and dashed into the wheelhouse.

"Great – let's get going. Is your rucksack packed? I've got the papers. We need the map, torches, food…"

"Oh," said Tash, peering into the darkness. "Wouldn't we be better waiting here until dawn? We don't know what's out there – what if there are dogs?"

Images of the bloodthirsty, clever packs who hunted them in the north flashed into Toby's mind. He pushed the memory back. "We can't wait, we need to get to the university," replied Toby. "Besides, we've got Snowy to protect us and there probably isn't anyone left for the dogs to bother hunting."

Toby didn't wait to see Tash's reaction. He ran to the cabin and started stuffing his things into his rucksack. There were some tins of beans and soup and a few packets of stale biscuits. Tash came in with her bag slung over her shoulder and started pushing a couple of warm jumpers into it.

"Put the maps in mine with the papers: it's waterproof," stated Toby.

Finally the two of them were ready. They stepped carefully onto the quay and set off across the cobbled street, following what looked like the main road uphill towards Edinburgh. Snowy trotted closely beside Tash, who had wrapped her wolf skin tightly round her shoulders.

"Do you know where we're going?" asked Tash, stumbling over a rotting fish box that lay in the road.

"We're at the Leith Docks, according to the map. We just need to head inland towards the city centre, but I think we should keep to the side streets, just in case…"

"Why?" cried Tash nervously. "What do you think might be here?"

Just then a strange guttural noise echoed through the night. They froze and listened intently.

"What was that?" asked Toby, grabbing hold of Tash's arm.

"Strange," she said. "I've no idea, but it doesn't sound friendly."

"Let's keep moving," Toby urged her, not wanting to think about what might lie ahead.

The two of them trudged on through the bitter night, slipping and sliding on the icy pavements, their head torches dancing beams of light in front of them. They slogged up street after deserted street, occasionally stopping so Toby could get a reading on his compass, while around them loomed the silent spectres of what had once been a thriving and busy city. Toby tried not to picture the houses and shops full of people living their lives: shopping, going to work or school, laughing and talking, unaware of the terrible tragedy that lay in the future.

Some of the buildings had been decimated by fire, their skeletal structures reaching upwards like monstrous blackened teeth. Shop windows, once full of fancy goods and food, lay ransacked and empty, staring out into the empty road. Rubbish was everywhere, blown and buffeted by the chill wind or lying soggy and rotting in the overflowing gutters. In some places, the festering piles of garbage had self-combusted and set light to wooden sheds and garages that were now charred, broken beams.

Toby and Tash soldiered on, aching legs and wet feet dragging slower and slower as exhaustion overtook them.

"Can we stop for a minute?" begged Tash. She was leaning on Snowy's wide, shaggy back. "I need a rest."

"Sure," Toby sighed, glad for the excuse to rest too.

As they caught their breath Toby shone his torch around them, throwing menacing shadows up the sides of the nearby buildings. Suddenly he stopped and trained the beam on one particular wall. He dragged his weary limbs over and read the bright red graffiti sprawled across it.

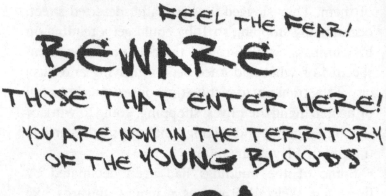

FEEL THE FEAR!
BEWARE
THOSE THAT ENTER HERE!
YOU ARE NOW IN THE TERRITORY
OF THE YOUNG BLOODS

Toby felt a sliver of fear chase down his spine.

"What does that mean?" asked Tash.

"I think that means that a gang once ruled this area," he replied.

"Are you sure? I... I mean are you sure they *once* ruled this area? How do we know they still don't?" gasped Tash.

"I don't, but that paint looks pretty old, and there hasn't been any sign of anyone around yet, has there? Still, I think we'd better keep moving."

"Ok Tobes," sighed Tash, letting Snowy pull her along.

Toby flashed his torch back up the street and illuminated, for the first time, what looked like a huge blockade further ahead. As they got nearer they saw it was a precarious tower of wooden pallets, old tables and chairs, all piled on top of two rusting cars parked nose-to-nose across the road. As if this wasn't enough to put people off, they had also layered the whole structure with a knotted mangle of barbed wire.

"Looks like this is the gang's way of stopping people from entering their territory," Toby whispered over his shoulder. "If they were still here, surely there'd be someone manning it. I think we're safe – just got to work out how to get round it." He tentatively shook the nearest plank, but nothing budged.

Toby swivelled round, shining his torch down a side street, but it, too, was blocked with burnt-out cars piled on top of one another.

"Looks like we've got to climb over it," remarked Tash. "Don't know what we're going to do about Snowy."

Toby stood lost in thought, then his face lit with a smile as he remembered something.

"Umm… I wonder if we can go through the houses?"

"How would we do that?" asked Tash.

"My dad once told me about his best mate, Andy, who lived next door to his auntie. When he wanted to go and see her he went through a little door in the attic, 'cos in terraced houses the attics are all linked up under one roof."

"Why didn't he just go through the front door, like everyone else?"

"I don't know – maybe it was just more fun – a bit like in *The Lion, the Witch and the Wardrobe.*"

"What is this witch and wardrobe?"

"It's a book. If I find a copy one day, you can read it – you'll love it!" Toby smiled. "Come on, let's try this house on the left." He led the way over to a brick-built terrace house at the side of the barricade. He shone his torch at the blue front door then stumbled back with shock. There was an official-looking notice pasted onto it:

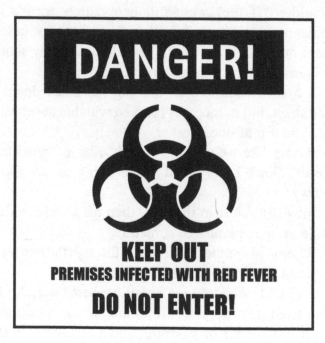

"Oh!" cried Tash just behind him. "Does that mean we'd better not go in? What if there are…"

"No," interrupted Toby, trying hard not to think about what they might find inside the ghostly house. "We'll be fine. Stick close to me and… just don't look in any of the bedrooms."

He turned the large brass doorknob tentatively, and gave the door a heave with his shoulder. It stuck for a moment and then gave way, throwing Toby forward to land in a heap in the dark hallway. Someone had clearly broken the lock already.

I don't know what we're going to find in here. But we've no choice; we've got to get past the barricade.

7.
ANYBODY HOME?

A deathly hush hung over the hall as Toby picked himself up and swatted away the sticky skeins of cobwebs that criss-crossed the passageway. A dank odour of decaying matter enveloped him like a blanket.

"Anybody home?" Tash called out into the echoing house.

Silence.

"Now would not be a good time to run into any of the Young Bloods," remarked Toby ruefully. "Right, let's find the hatch to the attic space."

"Maybe we should check the kitchen first," said Tash. "There might be some tinned food left, and some fuel; matches or something."

The two of them crept quietly down the hall, Tash hanging tightly onto Snowy's collar. Toby slowly pushed open a door and shone the torch inside. He hesitated; he didn't want to find the remains of whatever the red fever had done to the family that once lived there. But the thought of finding something useful drove him on.

There was a table in the centre of the room, set with knives and forks and plates. On a wooden board sat a misshapen lump of green-and-white fungus that Toby barely recognised as a former loaf of bread. Beside it was a dish of slimy, rancid fat that had once been butter. Next to each plate was a dusty rolled-up napkin held by a tarnished silver napkin ring. Toby picked one up. It had the letter S engraved on it. He picked the others up in turn; they each had a different capital letter etched into the silver. He thought of the family that had taken such care over these small objects – and who would never use them again.

"It's like they've just popped out for something," said Tash quietly. "The fever must have struck them quickly. They didn't even have time for breakfast."

"Yeah," murmured Toby. "That's how it affected a lot of people; healthy one moment and the next…"

"Let's not go there," declared Tash. "It's too awful to think about. Come on, we need to have a quick look around."

"Ok, you take those cupboards on the left, and I'll look in the pantry," said Toby, pulling a door open to reveal some shrivelled sprouting potatoes and half a pack of washing powder. "Someone must have been here already. There's nothing useful left."

"Same here – nothing. The Young Bloods must have taken it all," said Tash, closing the empty cupboard.

Toby shuddered at the idea of them rampaging around the house. "I don't like to think how they got their name," muttered Toby. "We'd better go and find this hatch."

The two of them slowly climbed the stairs with Snowy padding close behind. Toby flashed the torch over the cobwebbed ceiling and picked out a small wooden trapdoor. He stretched up to grab at the metal ring attached to it but even when he jumped up, it was out of his grasp. "I need a chair or something to climb up."

He glanced round the hallway and noticed one of the bedroom doors ajar.

I'm not going to look at the bed. Just look round the walls, there's bound to be a chair in there.

Trembling, Toby pushed the door open, his heart beating so hard he thought it might jump out of his chest. Discarded clothes and shoes littered the floor, along with an abandoned teddy bear and an overturned basket that had spilt its contents of toys. Holding his breath, and keeping his eyes away from the bed, he grabbed the first chair he saw and dragged it onto the landing. Then, gripping his torch between his teeth, he climbed onto the chair, jumped up and snatched at the ring.

"Got it!" he cried through clenched teeth. He pulled hard and the trapdoor swung downwards to reveal a metal ladder attached to the underside.

"Up we go, Snowy," called Tash to the massive wolf. "You can do this, come on. Hup!"

The wolf meekly placed his front paws on the bottom step and then, after a searching glance at Tash, bounded up the ladder into the black hole at the top.

"Wow, he trusts you doesn't he?" remarked Toby, following up the steps.

"He is good boy." Tash grinned. She climbed up behind Toby, coming to stand beside him at the top.

"This way I think," said Toby. "Need to get to the end where the next house joins on. Wow, this place is stuffed!" Bending down to avoid the low crossbeams, he threaded his way carefully between an old bike, some skis, a doll's house and a huge stack of yellowing magazines. He peered inside a plastic box as he pushed it aside. It was packed to the brim with Meccano, Playmobil, books, pictures and dolls. He thought of all his old toys lying scattered around his bedroom in the cottage at Collieston. He hadn't had time to pack them when they fled to the lighthouse. The only things he had taken were the marble eggs his mum used to collect, and his teddy, which was scrunched up at the bottom of his rucksack. These objects were all he had left to remind him of his mum.

Tash and Snowy caught up with him as he reached a plywood board nailed up across the end of the attic.

"I think this is covering the gap to the next house," he said, knocking on it. "It's only thin; we should be able to break through." Balancing cautiously on a joist, he swung his leg back and aimed his foot at the board.

CRACK!

The lightweight panel splintered and split across the middle. Toby staved it in with his boot, and squashed it down so they could get across into the space beyond.

This attic was surprisingly empty, except for a few broken toys and scattered jigsaw pieces, their boxes torn and thrown to one side. It looked like someone had already broken into this house and emptied it completely. Luckily for Toby and Tash, they had left the ladder down.

Snowy hesitantly followed as they climbed down into the main house, and looked around in horror. Every wall was daubed with red paint; graffiti and rude words were smeared everywhere.

"Seems like the Young Bloods have been busy in here!" exclaimed Toby, taking in the piles of dirty sheets, blankets and duvets that were scattered through the open rooms and the landing. They made their way down the stairs, picking carefully over broken glasses, smashed wine bottles, empty chocolate boxes, sweetie wrappers and cigarette packets. All around them hung the heavy smell of stale smoke and the stench of rotting matter.

"Not fussy about how they lived, then?" said Tash, surveying the ripped streamers of wallpaper hanging from the walls. "Here, Snowy, let me just check your feet for glass." She inspected each of the wolf's paws as he sat patiently offering them to her.

"I expect they just wreck one house and then move on to another. After all, they've got a whole city to live in," observed Toby. He was still ploughing through the decaying debris to clear a way for them to the front door, struggling to catch his breath in the thick air. As he stepped at last into the night he gulped in the cold, fresh air.

"Phew!" He was standing on the other side of the Young Bloods' roadblock. "We've got round it, Tash. Let's keep heading into the city."

"I'm so glad to be out of there!" exclaimed Tash as she stumbled after him. "And so is Snowy, aren't you boy?" The wolf looked up adoringly into her eyes and licked her hand.

As they neared the city, the desolation got worse; the streets were jammed with burnt-out cars, looming in the dark like skeletons of prehistoric creatures. Everywhere there were mounds of litter: cardboard boxes, newspapers, rusty tins, empty bottles. The tarmac of the road had erupted in places, pushed up by wanton weeds that had flourished in the decay. Young sapling trees had seeded in doorways and grown twisted and bent around smashed gates that hung off their hinges. Ivy flowed out of the gutters, waving in the wind like streamers, twisting and creeping through every crack in the walls and pavements.

"Looks like a war zone," said Toby, stopping to inspect another barricade – only this one had been torn down, the wreaths of barbed wire stacked against a tower of old doors and tables. "See, there," he pointed to a wall. "That looks like the sign of a different gang."

The wall was covered in blue paint, and it announced the presence of another mob: The Rude Boys. One sign said:

GIVE PEAS A CHANCE

"Don't they mean 'peace'?" asked Tash.

"I think they were trying to be funny," grunted Toby. "Come on, this place is giving me the shivers."

They trudged on, passing silent rows of empty houses that gradually disappeared into what looked like a building site. Forlorn-looking, half-constructed houses lined the unmade road, while huge diggers sat rusting in murky puddles surrounded by half-submerged bricks, sandbags and barrels. Scaffolding, swathed in plastic sheeting, ringed the edge of the muddy swamp. The beams of light from their torches danced over the billowing sheeting, throwing fiendish shadows across their path.

Don't like the look of this – it's a bit open. If we're attacked now we won't have a chance trying to make a run for it.

Suddenly Tash stopped in her tracks.

"What is it?" asked Toby, nervously.

"Thought I heard something," she whispered. "Listen."

The pair of them turned their heads to catch any noise apart from the shrill whining of the sharp wind.

"There, did you hear that?" cried Tash.

A low grumbling roar bellowed through the night.

Then another.

And another.

Then a high-pitched screaming sound filled the air – stopping suddenly, and leaving them in silence.

"Sounds like wild animals to me," hissed Tash. "Coming from up ahead towards the city centre."

"How is that possible?" murmured Toby.

The sounds came and went, travelling eerily through the cold air, getting louder and nearer as Toby and Tash stood transfixed, trembling in the cold.

That's all we need, wild animals roaming the streets.

As the clamouring calls drew closer and closer, Toby could feel the hairs on the back of his neck standing on end. He glanced down at Snowy. The wolf-dog's grey hackles along his ruff and back were fluffed up, making him look twice his usual size, and he was crouched low and ready to pounce.

He knows there's danger coming. Not sure even he would be able to protect us though.

"I think we need to hide, Tobes. Those noises are getting closer," warned Tash.

Toby cast around for somewhere safe. There were no secure houses within sight, but he spotted some large pipes sticking out of the muddy building site and dragged Tash over to them. "Quick! Get inside! Go on Snowy, follow your mum!"

Toby crawled into the concrete pipe behind them, shuffled in as far he could go and turned off his torch. Tash was curled up tight in front of him, one arm around Snowy, whose deep, wary growl grumbled in his chest.

"Keep him quiet, can you?" whispered Toby.

Tash soothed the wolf-dog, stroking his warm fur and shushing him in a singsong voice as he crouched, pointedly staring out of the pipe into the darkness.

The three of them squatted there, cold and shivering as the rumbling noises get nearer and nearer.

Wish I had some of that badger juice Jamie's mum made to put the dogs off her scent. Whatever was making that noise can probably smell us a mile off. Let's hope this pipe is too small for whatever's out there to get in.

Toby tried to still his breathing as the noises of something large and ponderous grew closer. It was sploshing its way through the muck and puddles of the building site, stopping every now and again to take deep sniffs. Tash closed her fingers around Snowy's muzzle.

Then there was quiet.

The three of them sat as still as statues while clouds of milky white breath filled the entrance to the tunnel.

It knew they were there.

There was a scrabbling noise as it tried to swipe inside the pipe and dig around the underneath of it. The creature reared up and bellowed in frustration, angry that it couldn't reach a tasty hot human for its tea.

The roaring, digging and grunting went on for what felt like hours, and Toby and Tash stayed completely still, but suddenly the beast seemed to lose interest. The splashing of its huge feet got quieter and quieter as it raced away across the debris-strewn streets.

They stayed stiff and silent for a while to be sure the danger had passed, then Toby breathed a long sigh of relief while Tash murmured sweetly under her breath to comfort Snowy. Neither of them could believe they were still alive.

"That was a bit close for comfortable," whispered Tash.

"Too close for comfort," whispered Toby.

"But I don't understand," Tash continued, "it sounded like a bear or something. How? Not even Snowy could fight off a bear. Could you, eh boy?" The large dog whined, wagged his tail and stuck his nose up to Tash's, giving her a slobbery lick.

"We'd better stay put for a while," said Toby, pulling his jacket close around him as icy fingers crept up his stiff legs and arms. "Try and get some sleep, since we're safe in here. We'll go to the university at dawn."

Toby stretched out his legs towards the mouth of the pipe and put his rucksack under his head, then wriggled himself into as comfortable a position as he could, close to Tash for warmth. Behind him, Tash had spread herself out in the other direction, facing into the pipe. She tucked Snowy into her side and cuddled up to him.

"Night," Toby murmured, exhaustion closing his gritty eyes as deep sleep washed over him.

8.
TERROR IN THE TUNNEL

"TOBY!"

Toby opened his eyes with difficulty. A gooey, sticky substance had gummed them together as he slept. He squinted as he peered towards the end of the tube, which was now suffused with a pale winter sun. He had been asleep for longer than he intended.

"TOBY! WAKE UP!" Tash was shouting at him, and then she frantically shook him, making his teeth rattle.

"What is it?" he gasped, struggling to move his frozen limbs. "What's the matter?"

"We've got to get out of here! There's something coming up from the other end of the pipe towards us," screamed Tash. "Snowy heard it first. Listen!"

Toby cocked his head and listened. A horrible scrabbling, scratching noise was getting louder and louder, reverberating through the pipeline. It sounded like many small but furious creatures were ascending towards them.

Immediately Toby beetled towards the mouth of the pipe, scuffing his hands and knees on the harsh, unforgiving concrete in his rush to get out – and to let Tash and Snowy out, too.

Just as they cleared the entrance, the deafening noise reached a crescendo.

"RUN!" yelled Toby, throwing his rucksack over his shoulder, and trying to force his cold muscles to work. His feet felt like they were nailed to the floor and his legs wobbled like jelly.

Come on Toby! Move!

Tash yelled something in Russian as she sprinted up alongside him.

Together they stumbled through the mud over strewn bricks and bags of cement, not daring to look behind them.

"What are they?" Toby cried, scanning the wreckage ahead of them for somewhere to escape the flood of the black creatures that poured forth from the pipe.

"Rats!" called Tash, breathlessly. She looked back to see them still spilling out of the pipe as she and Toby reached the line of half-built houses.

"But they're huge! Quick – climb up the scaffolding," yelled Toby. "Maybe if we get up high, they won't be able to reach us."

Toby glanced over his shoulder as he threw all his weight onto the wooden planks suspended across a frame of iron girders. The torrent of long-tailed vermin, their noses twitching, continued to spread out over the building site. They stopped momentarily, en masse, to catch the scent of their prey, then came hurtling towards the rickety frame on which Toby was now standing.

"Hurry!" he shouted. "Give Snowy a shove and I'll catch him."

Tash half boosted, half threw the leaping dog up towards Toby's outstretched arms. Toby just managed an awkward catch and hauled Snowy onto the scaffolding. Tash scrambled up after him, her feet leaving the floor just seconds before a scurry of slick rodents swept underneath.

"They're swarming!" puffed Tash. "It's like they're working together!"

"Yep," gasped Toby. "I wonder if they've been infected with the red fever like the dogs? The rats could have mutated to become more intelligent in the same way."

"But there's so many of them! Look – they're still coming out of the pipe. Maybe they aren't dangerous? Rats don't usually eat people!"

"Yep, but these are no ordinary rats, are they?" wheezed Toby, rubbing a sore stitch in his side. "And they probably haven't had any real food for ages. Probably full of diseases too."

As Toby and Tash balanced shakily on the planks, they watched the rats stop and reform into one gigantic swirling mass in the centre of the building site.

What are they doing? It's like they're planning their next move.

As if he had read their minds, the rats lined up together and started screeching and scurrying towards the scaffolding.

No, no, no, no! What can we use as a weapon?

Toby frantically looked around at the platform. It was scattered with discarded trowels, bricks and buckets. Nothing that could inflict much damage.

Then he spied a loose pole. Picking it up, he motioned Tash to stand behind him. As the first wave of rats breached the uprights, he swung the pole down, lashing at the ones that were zipping vertically up towards them.

Snowy lunged forwards too, barking ferociously at the encroaching attackers. Any rats stupid enough to come within reach of his slavering jaws were thrown over his shoulder to land stunned on the ground below.

"Climb up higher!" Toby called to Tash, shaking loose a rat that had sunk its teeth into the leather of his boot.

Tash grabbed Toby's rucksack and pulled herself onto the next level. Toby snatched Snowy under his front legs and propelled the dog towards Tash who, hanging precariously downwards, tugged him up beside her. Now the rats had overwhelmed Toby's level, he scaled the scaffolding a pole at a time, kicking out at the rabid beasts that continued to claw and bite him.

"Don't know how long we can hold them off!" he yelled, peering down between the broken spars to watch the ever-increasing swarm moving up the lower platform.

"We can't get any higher!" Tash shouted back.

Think, Toby! Think!

Just at that moment, a deafening noise caught Toby's attention. He looked up in surprise.

That sounded like a car horn. Can't be, surely?

"Look, Toby – look over there!" Tash screamed over the cacophony of scrabbling rats.

Toby stared out across the dilapidated site to where the works morphed into the city again. A large, shiny truck was bumping and bouncing over the rutted track at great speed. Barely visible over the steering wheel was the small, determined face of a young boy, deftly spinning the wheels this way and that to avoid the craters and pools. The vehicle crashed to a halt beside the scaffolding and the door flung open.

"Get in! Fast! Before these beasts chomp up my tyres." The boy threw himself out of the car holding a thick baton swathed in rags. He snapped open a lighter and held it to the baton.

Even from Toby's height on the scaffolding, he could smell the paraffin burning as the flames took swift hold.

The rats recoiled in terror as the boy fanned his flaming baton wildly around him, swiping out and beating a path to the scaffolding.

Toby and Tash didn't wait to ask who their saviour was, but hastily climbed down the shaky metal supports to land breathless at the boy's feet.

"Come on Snowy," urged Tash as the dog paced and whined on the platform, frightened by the roaring flames. Not wanting to leave his mistress, he took a giant leap and bounced down to the ground.

"Get in the car while I hold them back!" cried the boy.

Toby and Tash jumped into the back, pulling Snowy in behind them.

With one last effort, the boy flung the burning flare right into the mass of squirming rats and bolted for the driver's door, slamming it shut behind him.

He threw the car into reverse and put his foot down hard on the accelerator.

"My name's Hasif!" he yelled as they bumped and ricocheted backwards over the potholes and ditches, swerved round to face ahead and shot off up the hill.

"I'm Toby, and thanks – we were in real trouble."

"I'm Tash, and this is Snowy. How did you know we were there?"

"You were lucky – I was out hunting and heard the bear roaring – I knew he must have found something worth eating. I came to see what was on the menu!"

Toby blanched and looked at Tash.

I hope he doesn't mean he wants to eat us. What if we've been saved from one terror only to face another?

Toby had heard terrible stories of people being eaten in the desperate years after the red fever but had never believed them. Now he wasn't so sure.

"Don't freak out – I'm not going to eat you," said the boy, as if reading Toby's mind. "I'll take you to my hideout. Where've you come from? There's been no-one but me living in Edinburgh for months."

Should we trust him? Maybe he's taking us into a trap? Maybe there's a gang waiting for us at this hideout?

"How do you survive?" asked Tash.

The boy picked up a bow and arrow from the front seat next to him and held it up.

"I'm a hunter. See? There're loads of rabbits in the parks, and quite a few wild animals that escaped from the zoo. Last week I caught an antelope!"

"Well, that explains whatever was hunting us last night!" said Toby, nudging Tash.

"Yep, got to be armed and ready in these parts," said Hasif, patting his dashboard.

As the early morning sun bathed the city in a pink light, silhouetting dark spires against the horizon, Toby tried to get his bearings. The last twenty-four hours felt so unreal – how could they trust this flame-throwing kid?

If he slows down somewhere maybe we could leap out and make a run for it?

Toby tried to attract Tash's attention but she was too busy hanging on to Snowy as Hasif threw the large vehicle round corners, speeding up and down cobbled lanes.

It's no use – just have to wait until he stops. He's only a kid; maybe we can overpower him if he tries anything dodgy?

"This is Princes Street, isn't it?" Toby asked as they reached a wide thoroughfare. It looked sort of familiar, but the overgrown weeds and signs falling off the buildings gave the street a dejected air. He remembered it being alive with the bustle of tourists and street performers, businessmen in suits, and casual locals.

The park opposite was a wilderness. Tall trees and bushes had swallowed up the paths and benches where he'd once walked and sat with his family. From the south side of the park a great bastion of precipitous rock surged out of the greenery like a black volcano. On the very top were immense fortifications, their dark presence intimidating the street below.

"That's Edinburgh Castle, I've been there," gasped Toby. "And that's the Sir Walter Scott Monument," ιe continued, pointing at the tall structure now clarted white with bird droppings that oozed down its blackened arches. Under the arches sat a figure of a man in robes.

Hasif swerved to a halt between it and an impressive sandstone building. "Here's home."

Toby stared up at the elaborate façade with its arched mullioned windows, balconies, turrets, all topped with a fancy tower. He recognised it – it had once been a smart department store – but now ivy clung to the grimy windows and the gold letters on the front hung down dejectedly squint.

"Well?" Hasif hung halfway out his door. "Are you coming?"

9.
THE HOUSE OF HASIF

"*This* used to be called House of Jenners, but now is the House of *Hasif*!" Hasif laughed and motioned for Toby and Tash to follow.

Guess we have no choice!

Passing through the grubby glass revolving doors, Toby found himself in the huge former shop. Rails of clothes had been tumbled over, and mounds of jackets, hats, scarves and gloves lay discarded in what look like a giant jumble sale. Everything was covered with a thick fusty layer of dust. It didn't look like it had ever been home to a gang.

"The gangs ransacked the place early on," said Hasif, as if reading Toby's mind again. "But they didn't stay long – the food and booze ran out!"

"What did you do?" asked Tash.

"It was easy for a warrior like me – just kept hiding in churches and museums – places they didn't bother trashing. They were drunk most of the time and too busy fighting each other to notice me. They've probably drunk and fought their way through Glasgow too by now."

As the boy led them through the debris to the main

hall of the building, a small creature came rushing up to meet them, chattering incessantly. It leapt onto Hasif's shoulders and sat frantically pulling his hair. Hasif laughed at the surprised look on Toby and Tash's faces.

"This is Tally, my monkey. Her full name is Talisman 'cos she's my good luck charm."

"Oh, how cute," cried Tash. "Where did you get her from?"

"I rescued her," replied the boy. "Like I said, all the animals in the zoo broke free when there were no keepers around any more. They've just been living and breeding in the city ever since. The monkeys set up home in a park nearby, but not all of them were friendly. I discovered Tally one night, left all alone in a tree. Her mum must have died or abandoned her. She would have died too if I hadn't found her."

"So Edinburgh is full of escaped zoo animals?" asked Toby.

"Yeah, there are some nice ones like gazelles, antelopes and penguins, but most of them have been eaten by the lions and tigers."

"Lions and tigers? That must be what we heard in Leith," said Tash. "I thought the bear was bad enough."

"What about dogs?" queried Toby. "Have you seen any packs of big black ferocious dogs?"

"Not really," answered Hasif. "There have been some pet dogs roaming the city but they're not scary. They run away from me most of the time. Why?"

Toby told him about Aberdeen being dominated by the wild dogs, led by their clever and cunning leader, Cerberus.

"Yes," said Tash. "Our friend Jamie's mum is a scientist, and she thinks that the red fever has made them evolve at a faster rate…"

"But we haven't seen any since they had a battle with the wolves over Stirling way," interrupted Toby, not wanting to frighten Hasif.

"Well, I've had much scarier beasts to fight," announced Hasif. "Wait until you see the size of the lions. Mere mangy mutts are nothing!"

Umm, I wouldn't call Cerberus and his soldiers mere mangy mutts! Still, battling against wild animals can't be much fun.

He glanced at Tash, who had turned pale at Hasif's revelations. He smiled at her wearily – they had come this far, and the boy had managed to survive in this crazy city for the last few years, hadn't he?

Tash put her hand up to the fluffy-furred brown monkey. "Hello Tally," she said, stroking her soft coat. "I'm Tash and this is Snowy. He loves small furry creatures."

Yeah, for his dinner! Snowy had better not eat Tally, or else Hasif might want to use his bow and arrow on us!

They followed the boy and his monkey into a room at the side that had once been a café. There were plastic tables and chairs strewn around the room and a sign on the wall that read:

Bacon and Brie Panini   £3.50

Yum, I could just eat one of those, if not two or three.

"Hungry? Got some stew – you want some?" asked Hasif.

"Yeah, I'm starving," said Tash. "Can Snowy have some too?"

"Sure!"

"We haven't eaten properly for ages," said Toby, trying not to think about what might be in the stew.

Toby and Tash pulled up seats to the counter on which Hasif had rigged up a small camping stove connected to a bottle of gas. He placed the monkey carefully in a cat bed on a high shelf, lit the gas and placed a large saucepan on the ring.

"So, what *are* you doing in my city?" he asked, staring quizzically at Toby and Tash as he stirred the gloopy contents of the pan.

Toby rubbed his sore, tired eyes, then recounted their flight from Orkney, and how they had to find someone called Professor MacDuff, fast.

The boy looked at them as if he didn't believe a word.

"It's all true," retorted Tash. "I know it sounds crazy, but this whole world is crazy since the red fever."

"Yeah, you're right," said Hasif. "Nothing seems weird any more. Anything can happen. I didn't always hunt my food with a bow and arrow. I lived on an estate outside the bypass. I used to play with my mates on the swings and go for boat rides on the river. It was great."

And then, to everybody's surprise, Hasif burst into tears.

"It's ok, Hasif," Toby comforted him. "Warriors are allowed to cry too. I had a bit of a cry at my old house just yesterday."

Tash leant over too and squeezed the boy's small, grubby hand.

Hasif fished a hankie out of his pocket and blew hard into it. "You didn't see that, ok?" he said in a defiant voice.

"Nope, we saw nothing," replied Toby. "Let me tell you about how Tash and I escaped the Corporation, that'll cheer you up."

"Ok," said Hasif, sniffing heavily.

Toby recounted how he and Tash had snuck through the island fort's old sewage system to escape their former home, which had become their prison, thanks to the Corporation. Then he told him how Jamie helped them steal the *Lucky Lady* from under the soldiers' noses by setting off a storehouse full of fireworks to distract them.

This made Hasif smile. "Does your boat go as fast as my car?"

"Nearly," said Toby, blowing hard on the delicious-smelling stew the boy had placed in front of him.

"Yum…" murmured Tash through a mouthful of food. "This is tasty."

"Is it gazelle?" asked Toby nervously.

Hasif tapped his nose conspiratorially. "Secret recipe." He smiled.

After the three of them had finished their stew,

Toby pushed back his bowl with a sigh and looked at Hasif. "How about we help each other out."

"What d'you mean?"

"You know your way around this city – and you've got wheels. If you help us find MacDuff we'll take you back to Orkney with us. Then you won't be on your own any more."

"Poo!" exclaimed Hasif. "Why would I want to go there? I don't need ANYBODY! I can look after myself."

"We know you can, Hasif," said Tash persuasively. "But just think what you're missing. You must be lonely – there are loads of kids to play with on Orkney. You can't play footie on your own can you? And we've got fresh fruit and veg, and cows for milk."

Sounds great, Tash, but you've forgotten one major obstacle – the Corporation! If we don't get rid of them, none of us will be playing footie ever again.

"Milk?" gasped Hasif. "I'd love some fresh milk. I haven't had any for years. And I love footie."

Tash smiled and ruffled Snowy's fur.

"Would you really take me back with you? Or is this a trick? You just want to get your hands on my cars, don't you? You want to take over my city!" Hasif pushed back his chair and stood up.

"No," said Toby soothingly, "we *really* do need your help, Hasif. If we don't find this professor – if the Corporation develops a vaccine to the red fever before anyone else does – then we're all in great danger. They'll hunt down all the survivors and control the spread of the disease to take over everything. Edinburgh will become *their* city, not yours."

"See, it's not just us that need your help," added Tash, "the whole world needs your help."

Hasif laughed. "ME? Save the world? Ha! Now that *is* weird!" He poured some dried fruit and nuts into a bowl for Tally, who sat happily munching away, turning each nut over carefully in her tiny fingers before biting into it. "Can I take Tally?"

"Course you can!" said Tash, who had already grown fond of the little monkey. She reached over the counter and tickled Tally under the chin, stifling a yawn as she sat back. Snowy leant his head against her legs and let out a long sigh.

"So, if we have a deal... I don't suppose you know where the university is? I've got an address." Toby fished the crumpled letter out of his rucksack.

INFECTIOUS DISEASES, KING'S BUILDINGS, CHARLOTTE AUERBACH ROAD.

"I know exactly where that is!" boasted Hasif proudly. "I've been learning all the roads and buildings in the city – like a taxi driver. With all this practice I'm going to be the best ever taxi driver when..." He stopped and looked at the others. "Ok, so there's not going to be any need for taxis any time soon, is there? Well, it was something to do..."

"That was a great idea, Hasif – and really useful," interrupted Toby. "So can we go there now?"

"Yes, it's not far – about four miles? And no traffic to worry about!" chirped Hasif.

"Right, we'd better get going," said Toby. "Tash? Have you finished?"

Toby turned to find Tash asleep with her head on the counter, Tally coiled around her head like a fur hat, and Snowy slumbering at her feet.

"Shall we wake her?" asked Hasif.

"No, she's exhausted, and she'll be like a bear with a sore head if we wake her up now. We'll leave her a note."

I'm knackered too – but we must hurry up and find this professor. Hope she doesn't mind being left behind.

"Here," said Hasif, "there's a pencil and a bit of old card from a packet. You'll have to write it – I can't write, only read a little. Street signs mostly."

Toby had to stop himself from gasping out loud.

Can't write? What a numpty!

But then he remembered that when the red fever had swept across the country, all the schools closed down. Hasif would've been very young back then.

That's awful – I'd have gone barmy if I hadn't been able to read my books and write stories.

Toby remembered fondly the dark evenings he and Sylvie spent listening to his mum reading by candlelight. After she died, his dad was always too busy to read to them, so Toby took it upon himself to teach Sylvie. She would write funny little stories, mostly about ponies or fairies.

Poor Sylvie – wonder what she's doing right now? That Madame Sima better not have laid a hand on her! Don't think of that – concentrate on this mission!

"I'm ready," he said, pulling on his jacket, then

scribbling a rough note to Tash and propping it up on the counter. "Let's get going!"

"Going? Where you going?" A sleepy voice came from the tousled head of black hair, wolf skin and monkey fur on the counter. Tash looked up and stared at the two boys. "You weren't planning on going without me, were you?"

Toby averted his eyes and looked out of the greasy windows. "No, Tash, we were just about to wake you," he lied.

Crikes, I'd forgotten how tough Tash is. She'd be furious, no matter how tired she is, if we went without her. What was I thinking?

Hasif's eyes darted from Tash to Toby, trying to understand what was going on. He shrugged and said, "Come on, let's go!"

"Yeah," said Tash, yawning. "Come on, Snowy."

"And Tally," added Hasif. "She's great at letting me know when there's any danger!"

The three of them, with their dog and monkey, bolted the front door of House of Hasif behind them, and their new friend led them to a different car from the one they'd arrived in.

"Do you like my wheels? I've got tons of cars. This is a Porsche 4x4, XL Special Sports version… We'll take the A7 and down Mayfield Road. Should see Rankin Drive on the right hand side—"

"Ok, brilliant, let's get driving," said Toby.

Hasif kept on babbling while Toby half-listened in the front seat, thinking about what he was going to say to this Professor MacDuff when they found him. The envelope containing the precious research was tucked safely in his rucksack on his knee.

"Go easy!" he cried as Hasif skewed the car on two wheels round a tight bend.

"Sorry – thought you said you were in a hurry. Look, this is North Bridge – down there's the Edinburgh Waverley railway station. It's dead cool – loads of trains to play in. I even managed to start one once – couldn't get it to move though…"

Does this boy never shut up? Maybe it's not such a great idea to take him back to Orkney with us!

10.
KING'S BUILDINGS

Finally the car lurched to a halt.

"This is it!" cried Hasif. "University of Edinburgh, King's Buildings."

Toby fell out of the door and stretched wearily.

"Ouch, what's that?" He put his hand down to his calf, which had started to throb, then gasped as he touched a sore spot. He glanced down and to his horror saw a rip in his trousers, damp with fresh blood.

How did I not notice this earlier? Must have been running on adrenaline after escaping from the rats. Can't think about this now – Tash'll only insist we go home and bandage me up.

"Just tying my laces." He stooped to quickly tie a hankie round his stinging calf and pull the tattered trousers over the wound to hide it.

He then trailed after Hasif and Tash up to the imposing wooden doors of a large building with tall dark-eyed windows. The door was stiff, but like most places since the red fever, someone had already broken the lock.

Inside, the three of them picked their way over heaps of scattered papers and books. Someone had once lit a bonfire in the centre of the lobby, and the walls were now stained with old soot.

Toby studied a blackened board on the wall, using his sleeve to rub the grime from the lettering. "Here..." he said. "...Infectious Diseases are in the Ashworth Laboratories on the first floor. Look – the stairs are over there."

As they crept slowly up the stairs and along the deserted corridors, Toby could feel the hairs on the back of his neck rising again.

"Bit spooky," he muttered. "Are you sure all the gangs have gone?"

"Yep," replied Hasif.

"Still feels like someone is watching us," said Tash nervously, poking her head round the door of a large laboratory. Inside were more papers and books, broken glass beakers and test tubes.

Toby and Tash checked each lab carefully, but they all lay in the same state of disarray.

"It doesn't seem like anyone's been here in ages," said Hasif, standing at the door, as Toby methodically went through a pile of papers left on a bench.

"There's nothing here to help us," said Toby despondently.

"Let's try the basement," suggested Tash. "I saw a door in the downstairs hall."

The three of them trooped down the stairs, Toby trying his best not to limp from the pain in his leg. They peered nervously round corners and through doorways as they went.

The small wooden door in the hall was shut but not

locked, and led to a further, more cramped set of stone steps disappearing down. Toby went first, shining his torch in front as they delved deeper into the bowels of the building. They found themselves in a cavern with an arched roof and plain, whitewashed walls. It appeared to be a storeroom full of shelving, stacked to the ceiling with stuffed animals in glass cages.

"Don't like the look of this one!" declared Toby, staring at a striped badger whose glassy eyes stared back at him.

"What's this?" asked Hasif from behind a tall bookcase. Toby and Tash went to see.

"It's a dodo," Tash told him, laughing at the surprised look on the small warrior's face as he confronted a large bird skeleton on wheels.

"A dodo? I haven't seen any of those in my city!"

Toby and Tash both laughed.

"Well you wouldn't; they've been extinct for years," Tash told him.

"Extinct? What's that?" asked Hasif.

"What we'll be if we don't hurry up and find this professor," remarked Toby.

"It means that they all died out," replied Tash, ignoring Toby. "Mostly because of hunting."

"Oh," sighed Hasif. "That's a shame. I would have liked to have bagged one of those."

I hope he doesn't think he can go hunting our animals if we ever get him back to Orkney; can't see Dad being very impressed with that!

"There's nothing here either," sighed Toby, turning back to the stairs. "Tash? Where are you?"

Tash had disappeared behind a stack of shelves groaning with glass bottles full of yellowing worms and insects.

"Am over here," he heard her call. He squeezed behind the shelves to find Tash staring at a small metal door with a black skull and crossbones emblazoned on it.

DANGER!

No entry to unauthorised personnel
FULL PROTECTIVE CLOTHING MUST BE WORN

"Better not go in there then," remarked Hasif, appearing alongside them. He turned to go.

"Wait," cried Toby. "What better place to hide?" He tried the door but it was locked. "Tash, your keys won't work here, it's too modern. I'll get my crowbar out."

"No need, step out of the way," declared Hasif. He took out of his bag a matt-black revolver and a box of bullets.

"WHAT?" gasped Toby. "Hasif! What are you doing with a gun?"

"Told you I could take care of myself," replied

Hasif. "Needed it for protection from the gangs. Never actually had to use it though." He then expertly loaded the gun and pointed it at the door.

"You all go and hide over there!" he commanded with authority.

Toby didn't stop to argue with him but quickly snatched up Tally, grabbed hold of Tash and Snowy and leapt back behind a solid wooden desk.

"Cover your ears," Hasif shouted, squeezing the trigger.

"Hasif, st—"

The shot was deafening, and it reverberated through the low-ceilinged cavern.

The recoil sent Hasif staggering backwards, clutching his right shoulder. "See, easy peasy." He kicked open the bent and buckled door, which now had a smoking black hole where the lock had been.

"For goodness' sake, Hasif, you could have killed someone!" said Tash, comforting Snowy, who was whimpering with his tail between his legs.

"And now everyone within two miles of us knows we are here," added Toby.

"They'll never have heard it from down here," chirped Hasif.

"I hope so, for all our sakes," muttered Tash, caressing Tally, who was trying to bury herself in Tash's wolf skin.

Toby climbed through the wrecked door and into another cavernous room but this one was set out as a laboratory. Inside, it was clean and tidy with piles of neatly stacked journals on a bench, and a blackboard covered with indecipherable squiggles.

"Somebody has been here, and quite recently too," said Toby, running his fingers over the dust-free worktops. "But where are they now?" He limped round the lab, rummaging through piles of papers, staring at them, thinking that somehow they might hold a clue to the professor's whereabouts. He flopped listlessly onto a chair, trying to ignore the throbbing in his leg.

Damn! I was SO sure he'd be here, or there would be some clue or something. But there's nothing. It's hopeless. What are we going to do now?

"Maybe we should camp out here until he comes back?" suggested Hasif, polishing his gun on his fleece and slipping it back into the bag slung over his shoulder.

"What's the point?" sighed Toby. "It looks like he's tidied up and gone."

"And it'll be getting dark soon," mumbled Tash, dejectedly.

Toby hobbled back up the stairs and out of the building, stopping to tug at the makeshift bandage that was in danger of falling down.

He glanced at his fingers, which came away red. The wound was still bleeding. Toby stayed quiet and followed slowly after the others as they climbed back into the Porsche, trying not to show his discomfort. They could deal with it when they got back to House of Hasif. No point worrying about it now.

Hasif chattered non-stop all the way back to the

department store, recounting tales of how he had outwitted the gangs that had once roamed the city.

"...And one day I hid in the space in the ceiling in an office. They nearly got me that time. Wish I had had a dog like Snowy – that would've been cool. They would've been frightened of me then..."

Toby sat in gloomy silence, mulling over their predicament.

Where do we look now? Seems like we're on a 'goose's wild chase' after all. We can't go back to Orkney without finding the professor!

"Here we are! Back at the House of Hasif," proclaimed Hasif. He leapt out and danced towards the doors.

Don't know what he's got to be so happy about!

But Toby could see that, after years of struggling to survive on his own, Hasif was overjoyed to finally have company, even if he and Tash were a bit miserable.

As Toby pushed his way through the heavy doors of the store, he felt overcome with exhaustion. The world seemed to swim around him. His legs buckled and he collapsed to the floor.

"Tobes!" he heard Tash cry.

Come on, get up! Focus...

"On no! His leg. It's bleeding. Quick! Find me something to stop the flow!"

Toby was aware of the hot, sticky blood oozing down his leg, as someone ripped the trouser material away from the pulsating pain. Before he could ask how bad it was, the light inside his head flickered and he felt himself sinking into darkness.

11.
PLAYTIME

When Toby woke up he thought he must be dreaming. He was lying in a huge four-poster bed with red velvet curtains tied with red ribbons. He yawned and stretched. If only he could lie here forever, and not have to battle for survival every day.

Where am I?

Toby propped himself up on the sumptuous feather pillows and took in his surroundings. Night had fallen, but someone had lit candles round the huge room; the flickering lights danced in reflections on the dark mullioned windows. It *was* still the House of Hasif: and he must be in the furniture department. All around him were a dozen beautiful beds all dressed in smart covers and smothered in cushions.

"Hello," said Hasif, springing out from behind the bed hangings. His little monkey swung down from within the canopy to sit beside him. "So you are awake at last. We've disinfected your leg, and put on some of Tash's special cream. It's just a rat bite. It'll heal fine. I was tempted to try stitching it up, but Tash doesn't think I need to."

I'm SO glad about that! Thanks Tash!

"I... I... don't remember getting bitten," stuttered Toby. Something flashed through his brain about rat bites and disease.

Too late to worry about that now. I survived the red fever – what's a little dose of the plague to me?

"Where's Tash?" he asked.

"Shush," soothed Hasif, putting his finger to his lips. "She's fast asleep over there." He pointed to a pink heart-shaped bed, complete with frilly pink cushions and drapes. "She's exhausted too, specially after we carried you up here and dressed your wound."

"Wow, thanks!" said Toby, surprised they'd managed to get him up the stairs.

"I'm very strong – I lift weights every day. See?" The boy flexed his biceps. "Anyway, do you want to see my car collection? I've collected all the best cars in the city. Got a Ferrari, a Maserati, a Bentley, several Jags, loads of taxis... and did I tell you that I've got the car that was used in the last James Bond movie?"

"No you didn't."

"I watched it so many times with my brother. That was before... Y'know." Hasif fell silent. His bottom lip quivered.

"Hey, I'm really hungry," said Toby, kindly changing the subject. "What's for tea?"

"Plenty of stew left," said Hasif. "I'll bring some up."

"Thanks! It was tasty."

"I used to make much better stew with veggies from the Botanic Gardens, but something's living there now and I'm not sure it's safe any more."

"What do you mean, something?" asked Toby in alarm. "Another animal?"

"Yeah, I think there might be a pride of lionesses living in the Gardens. No kidding."

"Really? That sounds scary."

"Yeah. It's not safe to travel on foot any more. I lock myself in here at night, and go up to the restaurant at the top to keep watch. Nothing can get in here."

Yeah, that's what the raiders at Fort George thought, and the dogs still managed to take it over.

Toby sat up cautiously and tried his feet on the floor, wincing at the rush of pain.

"Sorry, no painkillers," said Hasif. "Young Bloods stole all the meds in the city."

Toby nodded and inspected his dressing: *not bad.* He was sure he couldn't have made such a neat job of it himself. He remembered the strange drink that his friend Jamie had made him once when his hand had become infected.

Could do with some of that right now, Jamie! I hope he's ok… And hope he's not too worried about us.

"Ok, tea time," yelled Hasif, bouncing on one of the many beds. "I'll go and heat up some stew."

Tally seemed to sense Toby's fears and jumped onto his shoulder, chattering into his ear as he settled himself back into the bed.

"Yeah, I know Tally, it's no good worrying. I'll feel better once I've got some food inside me".

Toby dozed with Tally on his chest until Hasif returned with a tray of hot stew for three. The boys sat in companionable silence near a still-sleeping Tash as they gulped their hot dinner down. Then Toby snuggled up with the monkey once more, and went back to sleep.

When he woke up again, Hasif was curled up on the bed at his feet, and Tash's pink bed opposite was now empty.

"Where's Tash and Tally gone?" asked Toby, suddenly realising that the monkey was missing too.

Hasif stretched and yawned, knocking an empty bowl off the bed with his elbow. "Dunno."

A short, sharp bark echoed down the hall. "Snowy? Tash must be upstairs. Let's go and find her." He gingerly climbed out of bed.

That magic cream of Tash's really works! My leg feels so much better.

"Tash?" Toby called up a tall empty atrium in the middle of the shop.

He trudged slowly up the wooden stairs, listening intently for any reply, with Hasif sleepily following. On the next half-floor he had to pick his way over broken bottles of perfume and scattered remains of make-up, jewellery, hairbrushes, handbags and umbrellas. Up some more stairs he found vacuum cleaners, toasters, kettles, food mixers, cameras, hair straighteners, and shavers of all shapes and sizes. All useless in a city without electricity.

Won't need any of those now!

Just as he reached the ladies' dress department, he heard a faint laugh. Following it, he found Tash knee-deep in a pile of evening dresses, running her hands over the soft silks, brightly coloured sequins and marabou feathers. Snowy and Tally were next to her, half-buried in the mound of fabric. The monkey was playing with a feather boa that was wrapped around Tash's neck.

Strange to see the wolf girl like this.

"How's your leg?" asked Tash, when she saw him. "I put some of my great-grandma's cream on the wound last night."

"Yeah, Hasif told me. Thanks, Tash. It does feel a lot better." Toby winced and collapsed in a chair next to her. "Still sore though."

"Look at these, Tobes," she said, turning back to the clothes scattered around her. "Aren't they beautiful? Much too big for me of course, but Mother would love them."

"And where would she wear them?" snapped Toby. "Is Madame Sima going to throw a ball and invite the islanders?"

"Tobes is cross. Are you upset about not finding the professor?"

"What do you think?" Toby sighed. "It's useless. It's like looking for a needle in a haystack. It was stupid of me to drag you all the way here for nothing…"

"Don't say that Tobes," interrupted Tash. "Don't give up now – you'll think of something – you always do."

"Yeah, something that will lead us into more danger," muttered Toby ruefully.

"Maybe Hasif's got an idea?"

"What, me?" said the boy, popping up behind a mannequin. "Ideas? I've got lots of them. Why don't you stay here with me and we'll rule Edinburgh?"

"You don't understand!" cried Toby. "We've got to get back before anything happens to—"

"Ok, ok," said Hasif looking offended. "Just trying to help. Maybe tomorrow we can start looking in other likely places."

"Like what?" asked Toby, still annoyed at Hasif's optimism.

"Like the castle – that would be a good place to hide! I haven't been up there for ages."

"Ok," said Toby. "What have we got to lose? Let's do that. Maybe it'll give us some more ideas anyway."

"What shall we do until then?" asked Tash. "We must let Toby's leg heal first."

"Play!" yelled Hasif.

Toby shrugged. He was too exhausted to argue, and he knew he would only make his leg worse if they were to go searching now.

"Come and look at what I've got in my House of Hasif!" shouted Hasif.

Together the three of them went up the stairs to the next floor, Tash stopping to scoop up an indignant Tally, who refused to stop playing with her new feathery toy.

"Wow!" cried Tash, spitting out feathers from the boa. "This looks like a treasure trove!"

Toby shone his torch over the large hall, and looked around him in amazement. They were standing in what must once have been the toy department.

Lining the walls were deep shelves packed with every shape and size of stuffed animal and teddy. Boxes of games and jigsaw puzzles filled the other shelves all the way up to the ceiling. Some of them had been pulled out and their contents scattered all over the floor. One large stand was totally covered with Star Wars figurines; another with Barbie dolls in different costumes; the next had hundreds of boxes full of Sylvanian Families in model windmills, canal boats, and a carriage holding a family of fluffy rabbits in dresses.

In the middle of the room was the most impressive build: a huge skyscraper made out of Lego, complete with surrounding office buildings, the London Eye, a castle, an oil platform, a quay containing a warship, and a set of Regency houses.

"Built all that myself," stated Hasif proudly. "Even got a working crane, see?" He bent down to show them.

"I always wanted the *Star Wars* Lego," said Toby, picking up a model of the Millennium Falcon, complete with figures of Han Solo and Princess Leia.

"I'm going to look at the Barbies," Tash told them. "I always wanted the beach one!"

Wow! Never had Tash down for a girlie-girl. Just shows you... you never can tell!

Toby and Hasif settled themselves down on the carpeted floor to make a Death Star. Hasif lit a hurricane lamp and placed it on top of a cabinet full of *Warhammer* figures. Tash disappeared into the shadowy recesses of the department and the boys could hear her telling Tally and Snowy all about the outfits she was putting on the dolls.

Time passed slowly as the three of them became lost in their imaginations, playing with toys they never thought they'd see again. Hasif ran excitedly between Toby and Tash, encouraging them to open more boxes, spilling the contents over the floor and sharing his treasures. Empty cardboard cartons piled up beside them as they played on into the night.

"Finished!" declared Toby triumphantly, carefully holding up a giant, shiny sphere of Lego bricks. "One Death Star. Now, where's Darth Vader got to?" He rummaged around a large mound of Lego men and women, pulling out the dark cloaked figure. "Here he is! All we need is the Millennium Falcon to blow it to pieces!"

"Let me!" shrieked Hasif, making spacecraft zooming noises. "Pow! Pow! Pow!"

Toby laughed as the imaginary missiles hit the Death Star and it disintegrated into a thousand pieces.

"Oh you two; only death and destruction will do!" mused Tash, pushing round a doll's trolley full of Barbies in colourful costumes. "Look what I've done."

"Very pretty," said Toby, but something Tash had said resonated inside of him.

Death and destruction... Is she right? Are we only interested in playing war games?

He threw the last of the Death Star down and

strode over to the large dusty windows down one side of the room. He rubbed a circle clean with his cuff and stared out into the darkness. Stormy clouds were scudding playfully over the waxy moon, throwing shadows over the imposing castle on the cliffs opposite. The wind was picking up again.

Where are you, Professor MacDuff? We shouldn't be playing games. We should be out there looking for you. But how are we going to find you in this sprawling city? And if we don't find you soon, all our efforts will be wasted...

12.
A SOLITARY SIGNAL

Toby gazed out into the night at Edinburgh Castle, which dominated the skyline, its formidable battlements towering over the city. In the half-light it reminded him of his first sight of Stirling Castle, where he had escaped the clutches of the evil General and climbed the walls to send...

"A signal!" cried Toby. "That's what we need to do. If we don't find him at the castle, we can send a Morse-code signal across the city."

"That's a brilliant idea, Tobes!" said Tash, throwing the trolley to one side. "It must be one of the highest points in the city."

"Cool!" cried Hasif, dropping a robot he had been making out of Stickle Bricks. "When shall we do it?"

"Now!" exclaimed Toby, excited that a plan had formulated in his head. "We need to go right now, shine the signal while it's dark."

"I told you you'd come up with something, didn't I?" said Tash, patting him heartily on his back like he was a good dog. "But let's do it tomorrow night and rest your leg."

"No!" said Toby. "Think of our families on Orkney

– they might be dealing with much worse than a bite on the leg. I'm *fine!*"

"Better take some ammo if we're going then," said Hasif. "The wild animals come out to hunt at night, never mind those rats."

"Ok, hunter boy. You can stand guard while Tash and I will do the signalling." Toby looked back at the many buildings that made up the ancient castle. "What's the highest point, d'you think?"

"Probs the clock tower on the Royal Palace," suggested Hasif, coming to stand next to Toby and peering across at the forbidding citadel. "Great. We're going to need a more powerful torch for the signal though – my wind-up one won't send a strong enough beam," said Toby. "Have you got anything stronger?"

"Yeah!" said Hasif. "I've collected all the torches and batteries I could find from the outdoor shops. Come on, I'll show you, they're in a store room at the back."

Eagerly, the three of them made their way to the back of the toy department, Snowy bouncing beside them, enjoying this sudden burst of activity. Tally rode on Hasif's shoulders, throwing Stickle Bricks at the excited dog.

Hasif opened the door to a large room shrouded in darkness.

Toby gasped as his torch lit up the hundreds of boxes and cartons piled to the ceiling. "Wow! You've stockpiled loads of stuff. Must've taken you ages."

"Well, I didn't have anything else to do, did I? I did it in the early days before the gangs really kicked off.

I did have more but they took a lot of it away with them."

"You were really lucky they didn't find you," said Tash, with concern on her face.

"Yeah, but I had Tally; she let me know when there was danger. She's a good friend."

Poor Hasif. He's had it even tougher than us. At least we've got our families and our friends.

Toby winced as he felt a stab of homesickness at the thought of his dad and Sylvie, and Jamie, and Katie, and...

"Here!" called Hasif, interrupting Toby's thoughts as he disappeared behind a stack of boxes.

Toby and Tash followed to find one end of the room was completely full of outdoor survival equipment such as tents, sleeping bags, stoves, gas canisters, batteries and torches.

"Need the most powerful one you've got," commanded Toby, "and better take spare batteries in case we have to signal for a long time."

"You've thought of everything," remarked Tash.

Hope this works, or else she'll just think it's another of my mad ideas!

"Let's get going," said Hasif, stuffing a large torch and several batteries into his bag. "I'll bring round a car."

"Hang on," replied Toby. "Just going to get something." He popped back into the toy department and re-traced his footsteps – carefully, so he didn't hurt his leg – to the Sylvanian Family stall. He picked up a box of tiny toy rabbits dressed in pink.

Poor Sylvie's never had many toys. She'll be over the moon with these… that's if I ever get them to her.

Toby packed them into his rucksack and followed the others down to the main entrance and out to the road, where the cold wind whipped their faces. The clouds had cleared slightly, leaving just the moon to illuminate the desolate street. With Tally on his shoulder, Hasif swung one of his black taxis onto the road and beckoned Toby, Tash and Snowy in.

Toby and Tash clung tightly onto the sides of their seats as the boy warrior accelerated round corners, swerving to miss a tram that had been left in the middle of the road. As the car climbed the steep hill towards the castle, Toby tried frantically to remember the Morse code he had used to summon the soldiers to Stirling Castle.

Hasif screeched to a halt at a crossroads high above the city and pointed to his left. "This is the Royal Mile. Down there, at the bottom, is Holyrood Palace and what used to be the Scottish Parliament."

Huh! Wonder what happened to all those politicians who tried to tell us there was nothing to worry about?

And up here…" Hasif heaved the steering wheel to the right and pulled the taxi up a steep cobbled road. "Edinburgh Castle."

The taxi bounced on, eventually coming to a screaming halt in front of a yellow barrier across the road. Ahead was a deserted esplanade that spread out across the front of a gatehouse huddled into the side of the fortress. The three of them piled out of the vehicle with Snowy and Tally in tow.

"You'll need to hurry. The animals will soon smell we are here," said Hasif, passing Toby the torch and batteries. "I've got flares; I'll fire one if anything's getting close. Watch out for rats…"

"Ok," replied Tash. "Don't go scaring us before we've begun."

Hasif shrugged and then climbed onto the bonnet of the taxi, sweeping his torch around the empty esplanade. Toby slung his rucksack onto his back and sprinted against the wind towards the buildings that towered above them. Tash caught up with him, her wolf skin fastened tight around her shoulders and Snowy trotting faithfully by her side. They passed through the archway of the gatehouse and stumbled up the cobbled walkway into the heart of the castle grounds.

Toby tried not to think of what may lie in the shadows thrown around by the movement of his torch.

"I've not forgiven you yet for nearly going to the King's Buildings without me." Tash grinned at him from under her wolf mask.

"Yeah? Well don't worry. I won't do that again. I need you with me."

"I know you do, Tobes." She leant towards him and squeezed his hand. It reminded Toby of his mum; she always used to grab his hand when times were bad. It was comforting, and he needed all the comfort and support he could get at the moment.

"This way looks like it leads up," said Tash, steering them to the left and then to the right, following the curve of the defences round and up some steep stone steps. Eventually they came out in a large courtyard surrounded by rows of tall crenellated buildings. On the west side stood the largest and most imposing of the lot, its lofty clock tower soaring above them.

"Reckon this must be the highest point, don't you think?" asked Toby.

"Yeah. Hey look, this sign says we're in the Crown Square, and this building is the Royal Palace," stated Tash, scanning her torch over a signpost. "Cool."

Tash got out her great-grandmother's skeleton keys just in case they needed to unlock the door, but as usual, it had already been broken.

Let's hope whoever broke in here is long gone. Unless it's MacDuff of course.

"Come on," encouraged Toby, leading the way through the door and up the stone steps that curled round inside the tower like the staircase in the lighthouse. A door in the first floor led into a room with a plaque:

FIRST FLOOR:

HONOURS OF SCOTLAND;
THE CROWN, THE SWORD
AND THE SCEPTRE
KNOWN AS
THE CROWN JEWELS
OF SCOTLAND
LIE HERE.

Toby peeked inside; the glass cabinets were smashed and empty; only a large pale sandstone block remained.

"What's that?" asked Tash, peering over his shoulder.

"That's the Stone of Destiny, according to this sign," Toby told her. "I remember my dad talking about it. It was kept in Westminster Abbey in London for ages. Kings and Queens used to be crowned on it, and Scotland tried to get it back loads of times. See, it says it was eventually brought back permanently to its rightful place in 1996."

"Just looks like a lump of rock to me," said Tash. "Seems like people were only interested in taking the gold and jewels."

"I guess the Young Bloods don't exactly care about their history," said Toby thoughtfully. "Not much use to anybody now, eh? Come on." Toby grunted and kept climbing the steps up towards the top of the turret. A small wooden door led them out onto the roof of the tower.

They stood, the winter wind biting at their exposed faces, and stared over the black mass of the city below them.

"This must have looked amazing all lit up," said Tash, ruffling Snowy's fur as he pressed his nose into her side and whined. "Right Tobes, I'll watch the north side of the city, and you signal to the south side. Then we'll swap," she instructed, positioning herself beside the battlements.

Nodding in agreement, Toby strode to the other side and flashed the strong beam of light out into the dark, flicking it off and on at differing lengths to alternate the letters of SOS:

... ——— ...

Over and over he tried, straining his eyes to watch for any reply. They alternated north and south, east and west, but no glimmer of a response twinkled across the quiet city beneath them.

"Anything your side?" he called to Tash.

"Nope, nothing yet," she replied. "Keep trying."

The cold air was seeping through his damp clothes, gnawing at his bones and stiffening his icy fingers.

"Oh, it's hopeless Tash! This was a rubbish idea!"

Suddenly the silvery shadows were lit by a brilliant pink light that shot high into the sky above them, bursting into thousands of small fragments.

A response? Oh no — a flare!

"That must be Hasif!" gasped Tash. "We'd better go!"

Toby started after her, still desperately searching the city for a flicker of an answer to his signal.

Oh, it's useless. The professor might not even be here. All we're attracting is rats and wild animals! Hang on though... what's that?

"Tash! Wait! Look!" he yelled, pointing out across the city. A small sparkle was coming from somewhere high up towards the north east.

"Come on, Toby! Hasif won't be able to hold whatever it is off much longer!" Tash screamed at him, returning to grab his arm and drag him down the stairs. The two of them half-ran, half-tumbled down the winding staircase, Snowy anxious at their heels, stumbling out into the bare and windswept square. They raced down the stone steps towards the castle entrance, swinging this way and that, trying hard to remember which way they had come.

"Not that way!" cried Tash as Toby veered to his right. "Down here!"

They followed Snowy's keen sense of direction down the slippery alleyway leading to the gatehouse. Sprinting through the castle's main archway, now in sight of Hasif's taxi, they became aware of a strange scratching sound just near them.

"What's that?" shrieked Tash, skidding to a halt.

"Dunno," said Toby, colliding into the back of her.

They shrank back into the shadows of the archway, holding their breath as the terrible noise gathered momentum.

What is it? Whatever it is, it's coming for us. Should we make a dash for the car, or stay here?

13.
CATS' EYES

The wind sighed and swirled around the ramparts, blowing dead leaves and spindrift across the cobbles. Toby and Tash hid in the shadows of a giant castle buttress, listening to the strange scratching noise getting closer and closer.

Suddenly Hasif appeared, running up the steps towards them, carrying his bow and arrows.

"I can't hold them back! The rats – there's too many of them!"

"Not again," croaked Tash.

"It's worse than that. I think they're running from something much bigger." yelled Hasif. "I had to leave the taxi." He ducked into the shelter of the stone wall.

Gusts of icy snow began to scatter around them.

"Let's find somewhere safe here," said Toby. He darted out and quickly retraced his footsteps back up the steps towards the Royal Palace, following the alleyway that was now white with a dusting of snow.

He waited for the other two to catch up and was just about to cross the empty square when Tash put her hand on his arm to restrain him.

"Wait!" she whispered. "There's something moving."

Toby squinted through the falling white flurries of snow – and then his heart gave a leap. In the darkness of the doorway to the palace he could just make out two discs of liquid amber staring at them.

"What is it?" he whispered back, a knot of fear tightening across his chest.

"Big cat," said Tash, holding tightly into Snowy's collar. The wolf-dog's hackles were up and a low rumbling was growing in his throat. He was staring intently at the glinting eyes of the creature opposite them.

"It's a lion," stated Hasif.

"Don't move," Tash interrupted him. "He might not be able to smell us in the snow."

Great! We're stuck between an army of vicious rats, whatever beast is chasing them, and now a lion!

The three of them stood trembling as the large shaggy-maned cat began to pad warily out of the palace towards them.

"Don't make any sudden movements," whispered Tash.

Toby and Hasif silently did as they were told, edging tentatively backwards into the gloom thrown by the buildings surrounding the square. The lion stopped and sniffed the air; he hadn't seen them but could sense something was nearby; something edible.

"Where can we hide?" whispered Toby, trying to keep the tremble of fear from his voice.

"Follow me! I've studied maps of the city and I know a secret escape route," hissed Hasif, feeling his way round the wall behind him. "We need to find Mons Meg – a big gun in the vaults."

Sliding silently round the outside of the square, they made their way to a low wall where a sign for Mons Meg was posted. There, a staircase led down to an iron gate.

"The gate's locked," said Hasif.

"Wait, I'll get my keys out," said Tash, rummaging inside her rucksack.

Thank God Tash has still got her great-grandma's skeleton keys – they've got us out of a few tricky spots!

Toby popped his head nervously above the wall. "Hurry up!" he hissed. "It's getting closer!"

"I'm trying, Tobes! Not making pancakes, y'know," spat Tash, fumbling with the large bundle of ancient rusty keys.

Just then a huge bellow echoed through the corridors of the castle, followed by the piercing screams of a thousand frantic rats.

"Yep, sounds like a bear!" said Hasif, trying to make himself as small as possible behind the wall. A small furry head darted out of Hasif's cosy jacket; the little monkey screeched with alarm.

At the sound of all the commotion, the lion stopped in his tracks, lifted his head and roared into the wind.

"Shush Tally!" commanded Hasif, stuffing the chattering monkey back inside his coat and zipping it up tight. "You'll give us away."

As they watched, the huge cat turned his majestic head in their direction and stared straight at them, his glittering eyes searing through the darkness.

"There's going to be a fight," declared Toby. "I don't fancy getting caught in the middle of it! Tash?"

"I'm going as fast as I can!" Tash gasped, struggling to fit a key into the metal lock of the barred gate.

Toby watched, horrified, as the lion shook the snow from his long tangled mane and slowly loped within inches of them. He held his breath and closed his eyes tight shut.

If I can't see it, it can't see me…

And then it was gone.

Hasif gulped. "That was a bit close."

"Yeah, well he may be back to polish us off once he's dealt with the bear. Don't like to think who's going to win that one!" said Toby.

"YES!" cried Tash through her teeth as with one mighty kick the gate swung open. "I'll lock it behind us; it won't keep the rats out but at least the lion and the bear won't be able to get us."

The three of them piled down the steps and into the cavernous dark below. Tash swung the gate shut behind them and bolted it.

"Where does this lead?" asked Toby.

"I think it goes under the Royal Mile and then down the Mound," said Hasif. "If we keep following it we should come out somewhere near Waverley Station."

Toby swept his torch over the stone-flagged floor and arched passageway. To each side he could make out small cramped cells where he presumed the prisoners of long ago were kept. Snowy led the way, sniffing the damp air as they silently trotted along until another gate appeared in the wall. Tash opened it with her keys and let them through.

On the other side, the passage grew narrower and narrower until they were feeling their way in single file along a low tunnel. Underfoot, the slabs were slippery, wet, and covered in moss, whilst green ferns and weeds sprouted from the dank walls. It seemed to take an age to grope their way along, the cobbled ground falling steeply under their feet.

Eventually Snowy came to a stop and whined.

"Another gate," remarked Tash, pulling out her keys.

After a struggle to get the ancient padlock open, they entered into a dusty cave full of the thick, pungent stench of decaying matter.

"Ugh!" exclaimed Toby, shining his torch around the dank room. "What's this? Look there're all sorts of manacles and chains…"

"It's… a torture chamber," said Tash, wandering over to the wall where grisly handcuffs and a row of nasty-looking devices were hung.

"It isn't real. Or at least not any more. This is part of the Edinburgh Dungeons attraction," said Hasif, pointing to a board with writing on it. "What does it say?"

Toby rubbed away the grime and shone his torch on the letters.

"Yuk! Sounds gruesome!"

"Wow!" cried Hasif. "There's even a dummy corpse in chains!"

Toby preferred not to look; it reminded him of what Madame Sima might be prepared to do to get the islanders to talk. Then, remembering the more immediate problem of the rats, he quickly led the way from the creepy chill of the cave and continued along the tunnel, passing other rooms where displays were laid out. There was even a full courtroom, complete with a dummy prisoner in the dock, and then nothing – except for an inky pool of black, stagnant water.

"Which way now?" asked Tash as they teetered on the slippery wooden jetty. "I think we took a wrong turning somewhere."

Toby shone his torch along the edge of the landing stage until it rested on a rickety old rowing boat. It looked like it could barely hold one person, let alone three and a giant wolf-dog. As they stood, reluctant to get in the boat, but dreading the thought of having to go back, Tally began to chatter.

"Uh oh," said Hasif.

"What?" whispered Toby.

"Get in!" Hasif pointed at the boat. "Quick! I told you Tally can always hear when there's danger.

Suddenly Toby became aware of the now-familiar noise of hundreds of claws scratching their way along the stone tunnel.

"GET IN NOW!" he cried, bundling Tash into the boat. Snowy whined and paced along the small jetty. "Call him, Tash. We need to go NOW!"

The scrabbling grew and grew, and as Snowy took a giant leap and landed in the boat – sending it rocking wildly – a black slick of writhing rats poured out of the mouth of the tunnel behind them.

Toby flung himself into the prow of the boat while Hasif, still on the deck, took a flare out of his pocket and lit it.

"Get back, you beasts!" he yelled, swiping the ground to the front of him as the rats drew level.

"Come on, Hasif!" cried Toby, frantically scrabbling to put the oars in the rowlocks. With one last swing at the screaming mass of creatures, Hasif shoved the boat and jumped in.

Toby pulled back on the oars with all his strength and the boat pulled slowly away. But still the rats advanced, jumping into the black water and swimming alongside them. Hasif sat at the back nearest them, swiping out at the sodden creatures with his flare still burning bright.

Snowy helped by grabbing any rats that were stupid enough to come close, and flinging them into the wall. Tash found a boat hook in the hull and used the metal end to bash them over the heads.

As Toby pulled and pushed, he winced with pain in his leg. He felt the wound rip open and blood begin to seep through the bandage. He tried not to think of it but concentrated instead on putting distance between them and the rats. As the boat picked up speed, the screaming dimmed to a low murmur that echoed through the tunnel. Hasif finally threw the flickering flare into the water.

"I think we've lost them!" cried Hasif.

"Phew!" sighed Toby, stopping to catch his breath and letting the boat glide silently on down the tunnel.

As they slowly floated along, the walls of the

overhanging cave made it impossible to row so Toby used his hands, griping tightly onto the slimy sides, to pull the boat along.

"Keep him still," pleaded Toby as Snowy bounded around, excitedly watching for any stray rats in the water. Tash grabbed hold of the dog and got him to sit quietly in the bottom.

"Here, Toby, let me take over," offered Tash. "Hasif can keep watch."

Toby gratefully swapped places and sat in the prow, watching the light from his torch bounce off the roof of the cavern.

"That was a bit scary," muttered Hasif. "Even for a warrior."

"I'll say," said a subdued Tash.

Better think of something to distract them, quick.

"Hey, this boat is called *King James*," said Toby, pointed at the now blue-green letters on a plaque on the prow. "I wonder which King James that is?"

"Didn't know there were any," chipped in Hasif.

"Yeah, well I suppose that's all stuff I learnt at school. Not much use now though, is it?" sighed Toby. The gnawing pain in his calf was making him feel sick.

"See," said Hasif as the boat approached another landing. "I knew there must be a way out from here."

"Well done Hasif – without you we would have been eaten alive back there." Tash carefully manoeuvred the boat alongside and slipped the rope over a wooden post, then leapt out.

Once on dry land again, the three of them made their way through an archway and out into a room containing only an empty kiosk and some dusty chairs.

"This must be the start of the tour you were talking about," Tash said to Hasif, smoothing the fur on Snowy's back. "Good boy – show us the way out."

She let the dog go and he bounded forwards, sniffing the air. After threading their way through various Victorian-looking rooms and passageways, Toby felt the stale air becoming fresher and cleaner. He never thought he'd be so grateful to hear the sound of the whistling wind again. They stumbled through a heavy studded door back out into the dark storm, and found themselves on a low street next to a large, garish sign:

"I reckon we're just by Waverley Station," said Hasif, casting the beam from his torch over the graffiti-painted walls next to the open door they had come through.

"How far to the House of Hasif?" asked Toby, feeling a finger of fear trickling down his spine.

"Not far at all, just right along here then up past the station and we're on Princes Street."

"We'd best wait until dawn," asked Tash. "We don't want to come across any more wild animals, not to mention those rats. We'll never hear anything creeping up on us in this storm."

"Yeah, I agree with Tash," said Toby, rubbing his throbbing leg. "Let's hunker down here in the dungeons – we can lock ourselves into one of the rooms and wait till it gets light."

They went back inside, securing the weighty entrance behind them, then made themselves as comfortable as possible in a room that looked like a scene from a Victorian street, complete with spooky doorways and gas lamps all draped in layers of dusty cobwebs.

Tash passed round some dried fruit and nuts she'd stored in her rucksack. Toby nibbled them slowly to make them last. His stomach churned noisily; it seemed days since their last dose of Hasif's stew.

"So, where next to search for MacDuff?" asked Hasif, with a yawn.

"Oh!" Toby sat up with a start. "Everything happened so fast I forgot to tell you! I think I saw a signal coming from somewhere near the city centre; it was high up. Sort of northeast from the castle. I know that's not much to go on but…"

"Balmoral Hotel?"

"No it wasn't a building, it was higher up than that."

"Calton Hill!" interrupted Hasif triumphantly. "Calton Hill – that'll be where it is. It's one of the highest points of the city, and there's an observatory there and everything. I've never gone there 'cos it used to be Young Bloods territory."

Toby shivered at the mention of the gang.

"We need to get there ASAP," said Toby.

"We need to get some sleep," muttered Tash grumpily as she snuggled into Snowy's warm fur.

"Ok, ok Tash," said Toby. "Here, Hasif, there's some cardboard boxes over there. Pass one over."

The two boys arranged the boxes around themselves and Tash as they struggled to get warm. But Toby could only stare into the darkness.

I'll never get to sleep. Too much to think about. What if we don't find Professor MacDuff on this hill? We could be walking straight into a trap set by the Young Bloods!

14.
CALTON HILL

"TELL ME WHERE PROFESSOR MACDUFF IS!" screeched Madame Sima. Her face was so close to Toby's that he could see the pores on her nose. Her black button eyes bored into his as she pinned him back against the wall. Toby tried to shake his hands free but they were manacled and chained above his head. Glancing round, he saw he was in a torture chamber. Along a bench next to him lay a row of shiny sharp instruments for extracting the truth from prisoners.

"You leave me no choice." Sima turned to her guard. "Bring me his sister."

"No, not Sylvie! PLEASE NOT SYLVIE!" Toby screamed.

Someone was shaking him now.

"Toby! Wake up, Toby! Wake up!"

"UH? What?" Toby shuddered back into the real world with a sickening jolt. "What happened?"

Tash and Snowy were staring down at him. "You were having a nightmare."

"Oh... it was awful," Toby stammered, shaking his head. "Madame Sima was threatening me. And Sylvie, she was going to..."

"It's ok, calm down," Tash gently told him, stroking his shaking hand. "We need to get a move on."

Tash is always so calm in a crisis. Wish I was more like her. I just feel so stressed out. She's right; we'd better get going to Calton Hill.

"Morning!" cried Hasif, coming cheerily in through the door. "Just been to check the coast is clear. It's snowed some more, which is good 'cos then we can see tracks in the snow, or a battalion of killer rats!"

Hasif's always so cheerful too! He's actually enjoying all this.

The trio packed up their meagre belongings and set off into the glare of the cold winter sun, the frozen snow crunching under their feet. Swinging right at the end of the street, they made their way past the grime-streaked and gaping entrance to the railway station, and on up towards Princes Street. The lowest point of this desolate road was littered with rubbish that had blown and collected here: wheelie bins spewed out their rotten contents and bundles of old newspapers somersaulted down the pavements like tumbleweed.

On one side of the street the overgrown park had burgeoned out through the crooked railings into the road, which were now rippled with ivy that crept up lampposts and hung in festoons from the overhead cables. On the other side, the empty shopfronts stared forlornly out, their doors smashed open and their contents lying on the pavements, covered with snow and ice. Stranded cars lay marooned in the middle of the debris, just as the Young Bloods had left them on the way up from Leith, while wilting weeds and trembling tree seedlings sprung from the cracks in the pavement and the tarmac of the road.

A bitter breeze blew hither and thither as Hasif led the way. They sprinted in bursts from one dark doorway to the next, always keeping their eyes and ears open for signs of predators. The silence was eerie in the snow, as if the city was holding its breath.

Much to Toby's relief, they made it safely to the House of Hasif without sight of a single creature.

"I'll go and put the stew on," pronounced Hasif, as they swung through the revolving doors of the former Jenners store.

"Are you ok?" Tash asked Toby as he staggered inside.

"Leg's a bit sore," he admitted, pointing to the bandaged lump on his calf.

"Let me have a look at it," Tash said, reaching into her rucksack. "You should have mentioned it last night; it's probably in need of some more of my great-grandma's cream."

Toby hobbled to a chair, sat down and tugged at his trouser leg. "Ouch!" he cried as the material scraped over the bandage. "That hurts!"

She must think I'm a right wimp. After all, she was so brave when she had that terrible tooth abscess and we were stranded on the mountain with wolves after us. She didn't cry once!

Tash knelt beside Toby and very carefully unwound the bandage to reveal an angry red wound oozing with thick green gunge. Toby winced as the last of the bandage stuck to his skin, and gasped at the whiff of infection that wafted from it.

"Oh," stated Tash. "Bit infected. I'll go and get some hot water to wash the wound." She dashed off to the café where Hasif was boiling some water in a pan. Within a few minutes she'd returned with a pile of clean towels and a bowl of steaming water into which she poured some green liquid out of a bottle.

"What's that?" asked Toby.

"Antiseptic. It's going to sting, I'm afraid," she said as she cautiously dabbed the wound with a towel she'd soaked in the solution.

"AH!" Toby gasped, bracing himself on the chair. Tash worked quietly and quickly, washing the wound and then applying some of the pink cream from her pot. Finally she wrapped a clean bandage around it and smiled at Toby.

"Thanks," he muttered through clenched teeth as the pain continued to course up his leg. Holding Tash and the walls for support, he managed to limp into the café and, though he felt a bit feverish and so not very hungry, he forced himself to eat a bowl of Hasif's stew. He didn't ask what the ingredients were; he didn't want to know.

"Perhaps we should rest today – go to Calton Hill tomorrow?" asked Tash, looking concernedly at Toby's flushed face.

"NO!" cried Toby. "We've got to go now – what if the person who signalled back moves on somewhere else?"

"I'm with Toby on this one," commented Hasif. "Best do it right now. I've just got to go and get

121

another vehicle from my garage. Glad we went in a taxi last night and not one of my sports cars – I would *not* have been happy to leave my Maserati for the rats to chew on!" He immediately left, carrying a handful of car keys. "Can't make my mind up whether to take the Ferrari or the Porsche…"

"I'm going to get some clean clothes, you coming?" said Toby trying to put on a brave face, though in truth the cream had already started to ease the pain.

Toby and Tash wandered through the ransacked clothes department, picking up the odd garment only to discard it.

"I remember Dad getting some really smart polo shirts here once, Ralph somebody's," said Toby.

"Ralph Lauren," Tash corrected him, as they searched through the fallen piles of rails. The smart suits were one of the few sections that had been left untouched by the Young Bloods. Open-fronted cupboards housed row after row of colourful shirts still on their hangers. Piles of trousers sat stacked by size, and towers of warm cable-knit jumpers lay exhibited behind glass counters.

"Ralph Lauren is obviously not cool enough for the gangs!" Toby shouted across to Tash, who'd disappeared into the ladies' department. He pulled down a royal blue shirt and peeled off his grimy layers. He put on the shirt and then chose a pale blue cashmere sweater and a duck-down gilet in navy blue.

"Wow! You look real smart!" cried Tash reappearing in a whole outfit of pink: jeans, sweatshirt and jacket.

Strange – never thought of her as a pink person!

"Er… you look good too!" enthused Toby. He had never seen her not wearing her wolf skin.

"Hey, you two coming?" A voice echoed up the stairs from the entrance hall. Tash and Toby both hurried down the stairs, accompanied by a very happy Snowy, who happened to be sporting a new collar and a spotty blue kerchief round his neck.

"Look at you!" laughed Hasif. "You might've washed too. Bit weird to be filthy in new clothes."

Tash stuck her tongue out at him, and together they raced for the sparkling sports car humming on the pavement outside, with Toby trudging behind, his rucksack over his shoulder

"What *is* that?" gasped Toby.

"That is a Maserati to you, mate!" Hasif giggled. He opened the door to show off the warm walnut fascia and cream leather seats. Tally was jumping excitedly from the front to the back, screeching with delight. The three of them squeezed inside the luxury car, which only just had enough room for Snowy to curl up in the back.

"Watch my leg," warned Toby as Tash squirmed in next to him. "Actually, you know what? It feels much better!"

I was worried it was going to go gangrenous and they'd have to chop my leg off. Thanks, Tash's great-grandma, for the amazing cream, I wonder what's in it?

Hasif was impatiently revving the car, the massive powerful engine growling under the bonnet. "Let's go!" he yelled over the roar as he took his foot off the clutch and the car plunged forwards, skidding off the snow-dusted pavement.

"Steady!" cried Toby, clinging onto the sides of his seat. The car zoomed along the white and silver-stippled streets, with Hasif crashing the gears and swearing under his breath as he navigated round burnt-out cars, trams, mounds of debris and upturned wheelie bins. Finally they could go no further: large stone bollards sat in the road, and the car skewed to a halt, spitting an arch of gravel and snow.

"It's not far from here. Shame we can't drive up – we barely got going!" cried Hasif, dashing from the car.

Tash helped Toby out and together they trudged up the steep gravel path. As Toby looked upwards he could make out a collection of monoliths standing like guards on the crest of the hill.

"Wow!" gasped Tash, pointing to a row of enormous columns silhouetted against the sky.

They carried on up the hill in silence, except for Snowy's soft panting and Tally's light chattering on Hasif's shoulder.

Nearer the top, Tash pointed to a squat stone building with a domed roof. "That round one looks like—"

"An observatory," interrupted Toby. "I've seen one before. The roof opens so a telescope can be pointed at the stars at night."

The three of them walked around the monuments, gazing with wonder at the dark shapes silhouetted against the bright blue sky.

"Eerie eh?" said Tash. "Like somewhere that ancient gods would be worshipped."

"Yeah," exclaimed Hasif. "Human sacrifices and all that."

"Oh shut up you two, you're giving me the creeps," said Toby. "Somebody must be here. Somebody sent that signal."

But there was no sign of anybody. No tracks in the crispy frozen grass, or an unlocked door. Nothing. The three of them searched the whole hill over and over until, exhausted, they sank down outside a turreted building that looked like a tall, thin wedding cake towering into the sky.

"This is the tallest building – the signal would most likely be sent from here," said Hasif.

The three of them moved cautiously towards its huge wooden door, which was studded with several modern-looking locking systems. Toby pulled at the large handles, but they wouldn't budge. "It's locked, and there doesn't seem to be any other way in. Tash, would your keys open any of these?"

Tash had already produced the chain of skeleton keys and was flicking through them, but not one of the keys she tried worked.

"It's useless," moaned Toby. "Whoever locked this place made sure it wasn't easy to get in. It's been done recently. And we're going to freeze to death if we stay out here any longer." He dejectedly rubbed his frozen arms and legs.

Why would they send a signal and then leave? I'm beginning to think I imagined the whole thing.

"We'll have a rest and then have another look," suggested Tash, fishing a nutty bar from her pocket and dangling it near Tally. The inquisitive monkey popped out of Hasif's jacket and sat on the step next to her, wrinkling up its tiny nose to sniff the icy air. Then, in an instant, Tally began to chatter excitedly and jump about on the grass in front of them.

"What's the matter?" asked Tash. "HEY! Where you going?"

The monkey had taken off across the grass and disappeared down a flight of steps around the side of the observatory. Hasif and Tash leapt to their feet and dashed after her. Snowy chased ahead, barking furiously. Toby followed behind, gathering up his rucksack containing the precious papers.

"Little devil – where's she gone?" cried Hasif, peering down the steps that seemed to lead to a cellar.

"Come here, Tally," called Tash, venturing down into the gloom with Snowy by the collar.

They all placed their feet carefully as they descended the icy stones into the small, dark cavern. Hasif turned on his torch and swept it around: the little monkey was chirruping in the corner over a small bowl of fruit placed neatly on the floor.

"Look!" cried Toby stumbling over the rough floor to the bowl. "There are peaches and grapes! I haven't seen them for years. How did they get here?" He greedily snatched up a ripe plump peach and bit into it. "Yum, this is delicious!"

As Hasif and Tash joined him they became aware of a shadowy figure blocking the light at the doorway.

Without any warning, a wooden slatted door banged shut behind them. There was a rattle of keys as someone locked them in.

"Hey!" shouted Toby. "HEY! Who are you? Don't lock us in! We've not come to harm you!" He squinted up at the dark form outlined by the sun streaming in behind their captor. He couldn't see a face but could only tell that it was a large person dressed in a baggy boiler suit.

"Let us out!" yelled Tash.

"Yeah! Let us out!" yelled Hasif, rushing to batter at the door. "You can't do this!"

"Oh yes I can," said an unexpectedly high voice. "I know you gang types. Can't be trusted. Why have you come back?"

"We're NOT from a gang!" exclaimed Toby. "We're looking for…"

"Don't waste your breath," interrupted the stranger.

The dark figure disappeared from the mouth of the cavern just as quickly as it had appeared.

Great! We're never going to find Professor MacDuff now – that can't be him, surely? Sounded more like a woman. But who? We can't be taken prisoner now – we've got to get back before anything happens to Dad and Sylvie!

Suddenly Toby had a flash of an idea, and he felt the hot flush of panic subside. It was going to be alright. "Use your skeleton keys, Tash!"

"Can't, Tobes. I left my rucksack by the tower when we ran to catch Tally. We're trapped."

15.
MONKEY BUSINESS

Toby slunk to the floor in despair, and buried his head in his hands. This was all too much: just when they thought they were getting somewhere with their search, this had to happen. Imprisoned by a mad woman, awaiting whatever was their fate at her hands. He felt hot tears pricking behind his eyes, and sniffed heavily.

"I should've been more careful. I should've known it could be a trap. I just thought…"

Tash slid down beside him and placed her small brown hand into his grubby gnarled one. "It's not your fault, Tobes. None of us saw this coming."

"Toby! Come and see this," Hasif called from the doorway.

"What?"

"That woman's gone and left the keys hanging on a nail in the wall outside. See?"

Toby rubbed his rough cuff over his wet cheeks and pulled himself over to the slatted wooden door. Hasif was right. There on a rusty nail in the wall hung a set of shiny silver keys.

"Yeah, that's great Hasif, but how are we meant to get them from here? Look, even with my arm fully stretched through the slats in the door, I can't reach them."

"I know," said Hasif, a big grin spreading across his face. "But Tally can! I've taught her to retrieve – she's a right thief and loves to collect shiny things." He picked a grape from the bowl of fruit they'd rescued from the hungry monkey, and rolled it carefully to just the other side of the door.

Inquisitive little Tally squeaked and squeezed herself gingerly under the tiny gap at the bottom of the door. Once through, she devoured the dusty grape.

"Fetch the keys, Tally!" Hasif threw a grape at the nail on the wall to get her attention.

Chattering to herself, Tally jumped up at the nail and snatched at the keys. Her first go was unsuccessful, but Hasif threw another grape and this time the monkey grasped the keys firmly and landed back down with them clasped in her paw.

"Come here, Tally," Hasif coaxed gently, holding out a piece of peach. He reached his arm through and tenderly took the keys from Tally's grip. He slid them along the floor and under the door. "Yes! I've got them! Now come back in, girl."

Unfortunately for them, the monkey was enjoying her taste of freedom a little too much. She had started to run up and down the steps, screeching with delight as the wind picked up, ruffling her fur.

"Shush Tally!" cried Hasif. "You'll bring that woman back! Be quiet and come here."

Tally sat on her back legs and watched quizzically as Hasif manoeuvred the keys through the slats of the door to try to unlock it from the wrong side. He couldn't get the right angle and gasped with frustration.

Just then, a flurry of freezing snow blew down the steps. Tally shook her silky fur and shivered, then decided that it was warmer inside the cellar. With one hop, she slid under the door and back into Hasif's welcoming arms.

He handed the keys over to Tash. "Here, you try – you've got smaller hands than me."

She slid her hand through as Hasif had, and tried to put one of the keys in the padlock. "It won't stay still," she moaned. "And I don't know which key fits. There are loads of them."

"Here, let me help," said Toby. "This one looks like a key for a padlock – the others look too big and bulky. I'll reach out and hold the padlock steady, while you put the key in." Toby pulled up the sleeve of his thick jacket and slid his bare arm through the gap as far as it would go, whilst Tash pushed hers up to the top where the padlock hung. He flailed around trying desperately to grab hold of the slippery cold lock.

"Got it!" he hissed, grabbing it between his frozen raw fingers. "I'll keep it still; you push the key in."

Minutes passed as Tash fumbled and fought with the key. "Hang on… just need to get it straight… yep! It's in, now for the twist…"

There was a clatter as the key clicked the lock open and it fell onto the ground.

"Yes!" said Toby, pulling his numb arm back through the slat.

Hasif swung the door open and the three of them cautiously climbed out of the darkness, shielding their eyes against the bright sunlight. Tash sent Snowy ahead to sniff out any signs of the woman in the boiler suit.

"What do we do now?" asked Hasif, snuggling Tally inside his warm jacket.

"Doesn't look like the Professor is here, unless that woman has him locked up too?" said Tash. Snowy was zigzagging across the frozen grass, sniffing excitedly and wagging his tail. Suddenly he started to bark in the direction of the Observatory.

"Let's go and have a look," said Toby. "Surely the three of us can overpower her, especially with Snowy on our side."

The other two nodded in agreement and they shadowed the big dog as he sniffed his way towards the huge domed building. As they trudged through the snow they slowed down, because standing in the doorway of the Observatory was the tall, striking figure of the woman who had imprisoned them.

"Where d'you think you're going?" she asked, holding out a large metal staff.

"Look, we're not here to hurt you; we're looking for Professor MacDuff!" cried Toby, trying not to sound as nervous as he felt. She surely wasn't going to attack three children? "Is he here?"

"Who wants to know?" came her gruff reply.

"We're friends of Dr Pettifer," shouted Tash, inching slowly forwards. "And his wife, Professor Pettifer."

There was a long silence between them.

"How do I know that you are not working for the Corporation?" grunted the woman.

Yes! She must know Professor MacDuff! Otherwise how would she have known about the Corporation?

"Can we speak to Professor MacDuff please?" repeated Toby.

"That depends."

"Wait!" said Toby, pulling something out from inside his rucksack. "Here – this horse amulet was given to me by Professor Pettifer." He held out the small dull bronze horse to the figure in the shadows.

Her gloved hand leaned towards him and took it.

"Do you believe us now?" asked Tash.

The woman appeared to hesitate for a few moments while she looked at the amulet. "Well, this is Layla's, but it doesn't mean I trust you," said the woman. She glanced up at the sky briefly and back at the shivering children in front of her. "Come inside at least and we can talk out of the storm."

"Thank you," said Toby.

The woman turned and stepped down out of view.

"Where's she gone?" gasped Hasif, rushing forward to catch a glimpse of the receding figure. "Look – there's a tunnel."

The three of them followed the woman into the low passageway that twisted and turned until they stepped out into a high underground cavern.

"Wow!" exclaimed Hasif.

Inside the subterranean hideout was a laboratory with benches groaning under bottles of strange-coloured liquids. Stacks of papers and books lined the walls, and in the middle there was a makeshift living area complete with sofa, stove, and sink.

The woman hung up her lantern, throwing an eerie light over the low ceiling above them. She stared at the horse and appeared to be gathering her thoughts, then held it up accusatively.

"How did you come by this? Did you steal it?"

"No!" said Toby, struggling to think of a way to allay her fears. "It was given to me by George Pettifer to convince MacDuff to trust us. If we could *please* just speak to him—"

"And *where* did you see George and Layla?" the woman interrupted him.

"On Orkney; they sent us all the way here to find Professor MacDuff because we need his help. We need to give him *this*!"

Toby delved into his rucksack and pulled out the research papers. The woman stared at them without speaking while Snowy barked and growled, disturbed by the tension in the room.

"You'd better tie that flipping dog up before it takes a lump out of me!"

"S… sorry," muttered Tash, holding tight onto Snowy's collar as he strained towards the stranger. "He doesn't like being tied up."

"And I don't think much of being bitten!" said the woman. "Now let me see these precious papers."

Toby hesitated. Did he really want to entrust a stranger with the papers? This was not part of the plan. As if reading his mind, the woman leant over and snatched them out of his hands.

She glanced down at the bundle, then frowned, pulling out the brown handwritten envelope and scrutinising it.

"Wait, this is a letter I wrote to George years ago, when I first started working on genetic manipulation of viruses," she said. "You couldn't possibly have got hold of this, unless..."

Suddenly something clicked in Toby's brain.

Oh! I get it! SHE is Professor MacDuff! All along we thought it was a man! How stupid of me!

The professor certainly looked like a man, dressed in a bulky boiler suit and clumpy thick-soled boots, with a knitted beret on her head. She pulled it off to reveal a much younger person than Toby had expected; her short blonde curly hair framing her cold-reddened face.

Toby lunged forward, grasped the surprised professor by the hand, and shook it enthusiastically like he was greeting a long lost friend. Tash and Hasif looked puzzled.

"*You're* MacDuff! Phew, are we glad to find you!" sighed Toby, screwing up his eyes in the harsh light and trying to get a better look at the professor.

"The question is, *why* are you trying to find me?" replied Professor MacDuff. "I thought George and Layla were dead or at least captured by the Corporation."

"They're not dead," burst out Toby. "But they have been captured – the Corporation has taken over our commune on Orkney and is holding everyone hostage. I think they came to capture you and the Pettifers, but the Pettifers thought you were dead too until I heard Madame Sima talking about you," ranted Toby.

This all sounds totally barmy! She must think I've gone mad!

"Steady on," said the professor. "Why don't you all sit down first and I'll get you something hot to eat? Don't mind the mess; I've not had any visitors for years. But I'm SO glad to hear about George and Layla!"

As the three friends snuggled up together on the sofa, Professor MacDuff handed them each a mug full of meaty stew she ladled from a large pot on the stove.

Why is it we always get given stew? Must be in a guide to surviving an apocalypse!

"Rat, is it?" asked Hasif, as if reading his mind. "Tastes like it – very good is it too."

"Yep," replied the professor. "Got a plentiful supply of them but they are a devil to kill. Giant beasts the size of cats – extremely clever too."

"Just like the dogs," murmured Toby, sneakily spitting out his mouthful of meat.

"What do you mean? Dogs?" said the professor.

Toby told her about the dogs living in Aberdeen, and how Katie McTavish had a theory about the red fever causing them to evolve to track down humans.

The professor's brow darkened as she became lost in thought. "Now," she said at long last, "start at the beginning – the Corporation invaded Orkney where you've been living... why did George and Layla send a bunch of kids to find me?"

"We were the only ones small enough to escape

through the pipes… and we've done some pretty brave things in the past even if we *are* just kids to you."

"Ok, ok, I'm sorry. Carry on." MacDuff smiled apologetically.

Toby went on to explain Madame Sima's interrogation, their imprisonment and how he and Tash had escaped Orkney. When he got to the bit about finding the research papers hidden in the ancient bible, Toby pointed to the papers on the professor's lap.

"George said you'd help us."

The professor started to scrutinise the writing. "Umm, this is very interesting!" she remarked, peering at the squiggles and symbols scrawled across the pages. She gave a quick bark of a laugh. "Seems George and Layla have discovered the final piece of the jigsaw."

"Jigsaw?" queried Hasif, stuffing his mouth full of the stew. "I thought it was a vaccine you were trying to find?"

"You noodle," quipped Tash. "Professor MacDuff means the last piece of information needed to formulate the vaccine!"

"Yes, indeed, you see I managed to escape from the Corporation's clutches before George and Layla. Once we knew what they were trying to do we had to flee. They must have been working on this after I left."

"Yeah," said Toby. "Lucky they kept it hidden so well from Sima."

Professor MacDuff was quiet for a moment, then she abruptly looked up at them, her eyes glassy. "I'm sorry to hear Layla hasn't been well – must have been the guilt that sent her over the edge."

"Guilt?" asked Toby. "What did she have to feel guilty about?"

"Didn't they tell you?" The professor stared pensively into the distance, her eyes filling with tears. "It was our fault."

"What was?" asked Toby, beginning to feel sick with apprehension. What was she trying to tell them?

"The red fever – the virus. It was the three of us that made it for the Corporation."

16.
THE TRUTH

"What?" croaked Tash. "YOU invented the red fever? YOU nearly wiped out everybody in the whole world?"

"I can't believe all this time we trusted the Pettifers..." Toby groaned. "I don't understand."

"You killed my parents," said Hasif, in a barely audible whisper.

Much to Toby's surprise the professor slumped down, her head in her hands, the tears spilling through her fingers.

"We didn't know, I swear," she sobbed. "We thought we were working on a virus to improve growth rates and increase immunity to disease in farm animals. We manipulated several viruses, made a hybrid... we didn't know that it would be deadly to humans, or that the Corporation was going to use it to control the population."

"What?" gasped Toby. "Red fever... created in a lab. My dad always said that it was a naturally occurring infection, like Ebola."

"That's what the Corporation wanted us all to think. Believe me, when we discovered the truth we worked like fury to destroy the vials and develop a vaccine –

and when we realised the Corporation wanted control of the vaccine too… we fled. But it was too late: they'd already spread the infection throughout the world. I got out first and I've been hiding here ever since, waiting to see if George and Layla made it."

"They told the Pettifers you were dead," said Tash. "But if there wasn't a vaccine, how did they avoid contracting red fever?"

"We were all working in the Artic where it is too cold for the virus to survive airborne. We waited it out, pretending we were working with the Corporation until the virus did its job across the world." At this, the professor wept.

The three friends stared wide-eyed in shock at her, unable to speak.

"But… but that's horrendous!" Toby eventually stuttered. "How could anybody do such a thing?"

"Well, they did… The Corporation saw their chance of taking over the world's resources. But it didn't quite go to plan; the virus stayed active much longer than they thought it would, and of course we couldn't develop a vaccine in time. When the Corporation found out how many scattered groups of survivors there were, we told them that they might still be infectious, hoping the Corporation would leave these colonies alone. But that's when the race to find a vaccine became critical; they needed to develop it before anyone else so they could immunise their troops and send them in anyway!"

"That's diabolical!" cried Tash. "And what happens if they don't come up with a vaccine?"

"They will – it's only a matter of time," warned the

professor. "They'll be getting desperate by now, and I'm worried if they've got George and Layla. Not to mention the islanders to use as bargaining ..."

"NO!" cried Toby and Tash.

Does that mean they'll threaten to kill them if Dr Pettifer doesn't do as they say?

"What will they do with them?" asked Tash.

"Well, perhaps use them to make the Pettifers develop the vaccine, I wouldn't put it past Madame Sima to use them as human guinea pigs in their experiments," said the professor, wiping the tears from her eyes. "The Corporation is not exactly known for using humane methods."

Human guinea pigs? This is a lot worse than I thought!

"We have to get back there, now!" cried Toby, trying to muster a plan, but thoughts were whirling round and round his head. Had the Corporation really let loose the deadly virus on the world? If so, it meant they'd stop at nothing to achieve their goal.

Toby jumped up from the sofa and made for the door.

"Come on," he yelled to the others.

"And what are we going to do when we get there?" cried Tash, sprinting up behind him, as Toby struggled down the dark passageway. "You can't take on the Corporation alone! It's madness!"

I don't know what we're going to do. It'll be impossible to smuggle everyone out, and even then, we'd never get them off the island. I wish Dad was here; he'd know what to do.

"I'll think of something once we're on our way, Tash, I've got to! Can't let Dad and Sylvie down."

"Wait!" called out Professor MacDuff, puffing and panting up behind them. "Now I've got the Pettifers' research I'll be able to formulate the vaccine quickly. You could try and barter with Madame Sima – say you'll swap me and the vaccine for the islanders' lives."

Toby stopped in his tracks and thought hard.

Barter with Madame Sima? That sounds impossible. But what choice do we have? At least if we can get the islanders to safety maybe we can go back for the professor once we find help? Dad will know what to do. Just got to get the vaccine back to Orkney.

"Ok, ok!" said Toby, returning to the inner sanctum of the lab. "You're right; there's no way we can go back empty handed. We're no match for the Corporation's storm troopers."

"I'll get straight onto this vaccine," said Professor MacDuff. "I know what they're like – they won't believe us unless we have the vaccine itself."

"What can we do to help?" asked Tash.

"I will take care of this, I know what I'm doing," said MacDuff.

Toby groaned and kicked the table in frustration. "How long will it take?"

"About twenty-four hours – it'll need to titrate overnight. Tell you what, if you want to be helpful, we'll need supplies for the journey there won't we? Why don't you go over to the Botanic Gardens and fetch us some more fruit? It'll take your mind off things."

"How are you growing fruit in the middle of winter?" asked Tash, letting Snowy lick her hand.

"I fixed up some wind turbines and solar panels and heated the greenhouses there. It's lovely and hot, even in this weather."

"In the Botanic Gardens?" asked an incredulous Hasif. "What about the wild beasts living in there?"

"Ah, I rigged up a system of speakers to a battery pack and CD player and recorded some lion noises, then played them back to keep the other animals away. Works a treat!"

"Well, it certainly fooled me," admitted Hasif. "Hey Toby, why don't you drive? That'll cheer you up."

Toby smiled. Typical of Hasif to think that driving a fast sports car would make everything ok. Still, he would quite like to drive the Maserati; it would make a change from his dad's battered old Land Rover.

☣ ☣ ☣

It felt good to be outside again; the snow had stopped falling and Toby breathed the cold air deep into his lungs. They strode down the hill, stopping to pick up Tash's backpack on the way.

"Do you know where we're going?" Toby asked as they reached the car.

"Yeah, I told you," replied Hasif. " I know my way around Edinburgh better than a taxi driver! It's not far – just go back on to Regent Road, left onto Leith Street, over the roundabout onto Broughton Street, then down the hill…"

"Yes, yes, we get the idea," said Tash. "Let's get going."

The small party, complete with dog and monkey, got back into the car. Toby's heart beat faster as he slid behind the wheel.

"Now," commanded Hasif. "Go steady. Watch you don't over-rev it; I don't want the clutch to burn out. You can corner really fast in this – sticks to the road like mud. And on a straight stretch you can reach speeds of…"

"There is ice on the road! I'm not going if Tobes is going to race," declared Tash. "Snowy won't like it."

"It's ok, Tash. I'll go nice and slow – to start with at least." Toby turned on the ignition and felt a thrill of power as the engine snarled under the bonnet. "Ha! Cool!" he called out as he put the car in gear and carefully let his foot up off the clutch. The car glided forwards, tyres throwing spits of sand, snow and gravel in the air.

Hasif was crouched in the back with the animals, leaning over to talk non-stop in Toby's ear about the difference between the automatic version and this one.

Tuning him out, Toby concentrated on the road in front. The steering was very sensitive; any slight touch and the car veered sideways. As he threw the car round corners, he glanced at Tash, who was gripping onto the dashboard with white knuckles. It reminded of him of the time they'd stolen a Land Rover from raiders at Fort William and he'd driven like a lunatic to catch them up as their convoy left the town. Tash had reason to be nervous: he'd crashed it into a ditch when he fell asleep driving through Glencoe in the snow. He was wide awake now though: how could he sleep when they were so near to getting the vaccine and going home? Plus, Hasif would never forgive him.

As Toby pulled out onto the broader streets and the road straightened, he put his foot down and the car surged forwards, throwing everyone back in their seats. He grinned, enjoying the buzz of going so fast as the car sped along.

"Whoa!" shouted Tash as they approached a roundabout and Toby had to throw on the brakes fast.

In no time they were at the gardens and Toby slowed the car to a halt.

"I think the greenhouses are on the other side," said Hasif as they left the car and wandered through the open gates. "Can't believe I fell for MacDuff's lion trick."

The once-manicured lawns and tended flowerbeds were consumed by weeds as high as Toby's waist. Tall grasses, stiff with frost, nodded in the breeze while brown, wilted dandelions, buttercups, nettles and docks lay rotting in plump piles dusted with snow.

"I remember this place," said Toby, studying the tall conifers that were still brushing the sky with their spiky branches. "My auntie used to work here, I think."

"I can see a wind turbine over in that corner; the greenhouse must be down there," said Tash. They skidded down the frosty path and found themselves at a large glasshouse sheltering in the lee of a tall brick wall. As they opened the door, a blast of warm, fruity air hit them. Bright arcs of light shone from the rafters, trained onto rows of ripening tomatoes that

144

hung in clusters from ropes of green foliage. A giant vine had wound its tendrils round supports, holding luminous bunches of heavy black fruit.

"What a fabby smell," exclaimed Tash, sniffing in the atmosphere.

"It's boiling in here," said Toby, unzipping his jacket and pulling off his gloves and scarf.

"Hey, what are these?" asked Hasif, plucking at the rich red berries half hidden among greenery that spilled out from a large earthenware pot.

"They're strawberries!" Toby laughed. It was easy to forget that Hasif had had a very limited experience of things from the past until now. Toby was glad he still remembered the last time he had tasted strawberries: his mum had picked them fresh from their cottage garden for their tea. As he popped one into his mouth now, he could almost taste the rich creaminess of her home-made ice cream too. Those happy days seemed such a long time ago. Before all this madness had taken over the world.

"Toby, you ok?" asked Tash.

"Yeah," said Toby, shaking himself out of his reverie. "Just thinking."

How does she do that? She always knows when I'm upset; I'm lucky to have a friend like Tash.

"Here, try these," she said, holding out a handful of soft raspberries.

"Toby, if your dad and sister are on Orkney, does that mean your mum died of the red fever like my parents did?" asked Hasif, following Toby's train of thought.

"No," sighed Toby, putting a hand on Hasif's shoulder. "She fell from a cliff when she went out to rescue our dog Monty from the wild dogs." An image of that terrible night flashed in front of him, as if he'd been transported back to the lighthouse, and could hear his dad's screams. "So, in a way, she died as a result of the red fever even though she didn't catch the virus."

"It wasn't your fault, Toby," Tash whispered, putting her hand on his arm.

"No, I know that now," said Toby. "But for a long time I blamed myself and thought my dad blamed me too," he explained to Hasif, then changed the subject. "Anyway, don't eat too much fruit. It'll give you a tummy ache, Hasif."

Hasif was halfway through guzzling a bunch of grapes, the juice trickling down his chin. "It'll be worth it," he mumbled through a mouthful of juicy pulp.

"We'd better get back," announced Tash. "It'll be dark soon and I'd rather not meet any more lions or bears tonight."

"Ok," said Toby. "Let's take it back to the professor."

Once they had carefully packed their bags with as much fruit as they could carry, they made their way to the car.

"Don't get any juice on the seats," Hasif warned. "Don't want the leather to get stained."

"Oh, you and this blinking car!" exclaimed Tash, squeezing herself and Snowy into the passenger seat.

Toby drove sedately back to the Observatory, aware of their precious cargo of squishable fruit. The sky was washed with painterly pink streaks as the night crept over the city, and a cold frost bit at their fingers and toes as they humped their bags back up Calton Hill.

"Hello!" called out Professor MacDuff as they entered the sparsely lit chamber. They found her bent over a glittering array of test tubes and flasks, mixing up some concoction of multi-coloured fluids. "Good news! We've cracked it! Thank God the Pettifers got their findings to my lab. All I've got to do now is leave it overnight to triple titrate and we'll have a sample of the vaccine to trade."

"Yes!" cried the trio in unison.

Great. Now all we've got to do is make the dangerous journey back to Orkney, convince Madame Sima to let Dad and the islanders go, and then rescue MacDuff, George and Layla. Then what?

17.
RACING HOME

Toby, Tash and Hasif spent the night on MacDuff's old sagging sofas. They had pulled them up close to the stove, which gave off the only warmth in the room. All through the night, Toby tossed and turned, worries and fears flitting through his brain.

What would they find when they got back to Orkney? Had Madame Sima's team already started experimenting on his dad and Sylvie? What if Madame Sima won't trade MacDuff for them? And what if they couldn't fight the Corporation afterwards?

When he woke, Toby decided that the adults could worry about all that. All he had to do was get the professor and the vaccine to the island. That would be hard enough.

"Tobes, you awake?" asked a sleepy Tash, peeking out of her blankets next to him. "The professor's been up for ages, packing stuff."

Toby and Tash woke Hasif, who was sleeping like a baby, cuddled up with Tally. Professor MacDuff laid out plenty of fruit, some yoghurt made from powdered baby milk, and some drop scones fresh from the top of the stove.

After a quick splash of cold water and a rub of his teeth, Toby was packed and ready to move.

"Ok! Are we all ready?" asked Professor MacDuff, appearing in a clean, green boiler suit and walking boots, carrying a medical-grade holdall. "Where's Hasif?"

"He went to get another vehicle," Tash informed her. "We can't all get in his silly Maserati so he's driven to his garage to get a 4x4."

As they locked up the Observatory, Tash smiled at her bag of fresh apples. "You know, we should try growing our own fruit like this on the island."

"Umm, we have some more important things to be worrying about, Tash," muttered Toby, his mind on getting to the *Lucky Lady*.

What if we can't find her? What if she'd been stolen or vandalised by the gangs?

"Yes, I know," continued Tash, "but if we had more wind turbines, and…"

"Don't bother me about that now," snapped Toby. "I've got to get us there first!"

"It's ok, Tobes, don't worry." Tash took his hand as they started down the hill. "We've come through worse than this, remember?"

Toby instantly regretted being so harsh. After all, Tash was on his side.

As they reached the bollards at the bottom of the hill, Hasif screeched up in a sleek grey Hummer with black-tinted windows.

"It's got a top-of-the-range, in-house audio system with eight speakers and Bluetooth!" he announced as he opened the door.

"Not much use now," commented Toby.

"Oh, I don't know. Listen to this!" cried Hasif. "Found these old CDs in a shop on Princes Street. What d'you think?" He turned up the volume and the throbbing bass of rock music blared out.

"Can't we have something less… well, less noisy?" asked Professor MacDuff. Hasif rummaged about in the glove compartment before stuffing a new CD into the machine. "Now this is stirring stuff; more your thing, Prof!"

"Ah, Tchaikovsky's *1812 Overture*. I haven't heard it for years," Professor MacDuff laughed.

"When I drive around I always put on classical stuff. It's great to race to!" Hasif declared.

In the back of the car with Tash and Snowy, Toby found himself smiling at the image of Hasif driving his open-topped sport cars around the deserted city, hair streaming in the breeze, singing along to old masterpieces.

"You said Leith Docks, didn't you Toby?" asked Hasif, expertly swinging the car onto the main road.

"I think so, yeah. Near the *Royal Yacht Britannia*."

"That's easy peasy – straight down Leith Walk and we're there."

Within minutes they had arrived at the desolate docks, where rusting cranes stood in rows like huge dozing birds beside the sea. Towers of large metal containers, corroding in the salty air, dwarfed a mound of small boats that had washed up on the quayside. Among the stacks of scrap metal that had once been someone's pride and joy floated the majestic *Royal Yacht*

Britannia, her funnels stretching to the sky. Tethered at the opposite dock, was the *Lucky Lady*.

Toby felt a wave of relief wash over him at the familiar sight of the little boat. He felt his spirits lift at the thought of being back on the high seas. At least then he could feel in control.

Hasif braked sharply on the quayside and they all clambered out of the car.

"You cast off, Tash, while I start the engine," ordered Toby, jumping onto the boat's deck. "Everyone else, hop in."

"Aye aye, Tobes!" shouted Tash, pulling the thick skein of rope off a bollard and throwing it onto the deck. As the engine leapt into life with a roar, the professor went to stow her precious cargo in the cabin. Tash and Snowy nimbly jumped down and joined the two boys in the wheelhouse.

At last Toby swung the *Lucky Lady* away from the quay. "Grab that map, will you?"

Tash knew the one he needed; they'd been working together for a long time now. She laid it beside the steering wheel.

"We're best to head out East to give the coast a wide berth," said Toby, squinting at the map. "Don't want to hit any rocky outcrops."

As the boat left the calm waters of the harbour the firth turned choppy. Toby braced himself against the wheel as the *Lucky Lady* pitched and rolled in the surging swell.

"You couldn't check that the hatches are battened down, could you Hasif?" he asked.

"Err, err… well… I don't feel so good…" stuttered Hasif. Toby glanced round and was alarmed to see the younger boy had turned a strange, pale green colour and was clutching his stomach.

Suddenly Hasif gave a great gulp and dashed for the door.

"Make sure you're sick downwind!" called Tash, following him outside. "Whoops! Too late! Looks like he got a face full!"

"Yuk!" said Toby, remembering all the times he had been seasick when he and his dad had first gone sailing.

"I'll check the hatches then," said Tash, heading outside. Toby concentrated on the dark blue sea that dipped and danced around them.

Hope the weather doesn't turn nasty. That's all we need – another storm.

Before long, Tash returned. "That's everything secured."

"Thanks," replied Toby. "How's Hasif?"

"Oh, you'd think he was dying," said Tash, laughing. "He's cuddled up on Sylvie's bed with Tally!"

"Haha!" remarked Toby. "He'll have to get used to it; we've got a long journey ahead."

"Do you want me to stay and keep you company?" asked Tash.

"Yep, if you wouldn't mind," said Toby. "Don't want to hit the rocks again."

As the small boat battled on Toby tried to work out from their speed where they were.

Should be just reaching the Fife coast now. Feels like the wind is picking up. Best not to get too far out in the open seas. Whoa! What was that?

A monstrous wave slapped hard against the port side, sending the boat surging the other way. Something was throbbing beneath their feet, the vibrations travelling through the floor of the wheelhouse.

What is going on? An earthquake under the sea? Or a deep-sea monster? Maybe it's one of those killer whales!

"What *is* that?" asked Tash anxiously.

"I don't know – better go and have a look."

Then the *Lucky Lady* gave a judder and trembled as if it had been hit by a tidal wave. Toby felt his stomach tighten, a knot of fear gripping his throat as if trying to strangle him.

He left the wheelhouse and stared out across the angry grey-blue sea. The winter sun glistened weakly off the disturbed waves. To the left he could just make out a nest of cottages huddled on a hillside, to the right the open sea stretched into the distance, but to the front a deep furrow of menacing surf was rising in the middle of a foaming channel.

Something is surfacing – but what?

Toby clung onto the deck rails, mesmerised by the sight in front of him. An enormous grey shape, like a monstrous metal whale, emerged from the troubled surf.

Help! It's gigantic! That's no ordinary vessel, that's a nuclear submarine!

Toby had seen pictures of such subs in some of his dad's engineering magazines, but never had he seen anything so huge up close.

After the square tower on top of the sub came into full view, draining seawater from its sides, the rest of the huge sleek tube appeared, dwarfing *Lady*. The little boat rocked violently as a huge wave surged away from it and thwacked hard against the hull, soaking Toby and knocking him off his feet.

The Corporation has come to kill us! We're going to be capsized!

Toby forced himself into action. "Tash! Get your lifebelt on! I'll get Hasif and the Professor."

Toby snatched up a couple of life jackets and raced into the cabin.

"What's going on?" shouted MacDuff, her eyes wide with panic.

"Get these on!" Toby shouted back, throwing her a jacket, and shaking the groaning Hasif, who was lying with his hands over his head on the bunk bed.

The professor flung on the jacket, swung her holdall over her shoulder and sprinted to the door.

"Hasif! Get up!" Toby yelled. "The Corporation has sent a submarine to get us! WE NEED TO GET OFF THE BOAT NOW!"

"What?" Hasif groaned. "I can't move."

Toby dragged Hasif off the bed, stuffed a life jacket over his head and pulled him out of the cabin after him. Tash and Snowy were already at the stern unloading the tiny emergency dinghy.

"Get in!" Toby had to shout above the sound of the roaring waves that were crashing on the deck.

Professor MacDuff and Tash climbed into the dinghy, which was already bucking and bouncing in the churning seas. Snowy followed, and Hasif clambered after them, frantically zipping Tally into his jacket. Toby untied the rope, threw it into the small craft and jumped down to land heavily between the others.

"Grab those!" He pointed to the wooden oars lying on the bottom of the boat, ordering whoever in the boat that would listen. "Give me one, you stick one in the rowlock and ROW!"

Professor MacDuff did as she was told and wrestled a long oar into the sea. Toby put all his weight behind his own oar.

If Lady *goes down we might get sucked down with her! Move, move, move!*

Just as their little dinghy began to move away, a giant wave crashed against the side of *Lady*, slamming her stern into them.

"Oh my god," cried Tash, glancing up at the huge grey submarine that loomed over them and their abandoned boat. "It's massive!"

"Head for the coast," yelled Toby. "It won't be able to reach the shallower waters. Tash, try to start the motor!"

Tash yanked the cord with all her might, again and again, but the motor wouldn't start. As Toby and MacDuff's rowing pulled them away from the sub, Toby spotted something that filled his heart with dread. A reef of black rocks stuck out into the channel and the current was dragging them towards it.

"Pull harder!" he cried, frantically rowing. He could see that Tash was putting everything she could into starting the motor, but it stayed dead. The wee boat bobbed ineffectually in the wake of the sub, thrown this way and that, and all the time getting closer and closer to the angry sharp teeth of the reef—

CRACK!

There was a sickening splintering noise as the dinghy's wooden planks were ripped like paper on the jagged rocks. Water flooded in, washing Toby and the others over the side. He tried to grab hold of Tash, but in a burst of foam the sea had pulled her from his grasp. All around them, the choppy waters were awash with the sharp, broken spars of the boat. He flailed out with his arms, trying to catch something to hang on to as another wave threw him nearer the deadly rocks.

Can I swim to shore? Can I jump onto the reef? Where are the others?

But before he could make a decision, another wave slapped something solid against his head. He felt himself slipping into darkness, a darkness from which there would be no coming back. The cold waters slipped over his head and down, down he sank, under the white froth of the waves and into the jagged reef.

The last thoughts in his head were those of Sylvie and his dad.

I'm sorry, I've let you down.

18.
A RIGHT ROYAL SURPRISE

Slipping in and out of the darkness of unconsciousness, Toby became aware of something pulling at him. He managed to half-open one eye through the sting of saltwater and was met with a strange sight. It looked like a seal with a huge pair of goggles on. It felt like a seal too as Toby reached out to feel its shiny black skin. But as he touched it he realised exactly what it was. It was a diver.

Opening both eyes, Toby could see some yellow oxygen canisters strapped to the back of this man-seal. The diver motioned with his gloved hands towards a dark shadow that hung over them. He squinted up and saw that he had been dragged towards the submarine, which loomed like a fat, round whale high above them.

I don't want to go there. But I'm not going to be able to get away from him.

The bump on his head and the lack of oxygen was making him feel woozy and sick. Toby grabbed hold of the base of a metal ladder and suddenly, from above, a pair of strong arms was lifting him. Toby's limp body was slowly raised up the side of the sub.

"Where are the others?" he gasped into the face of the diver who stared impassively back.

As he was shoved over to the main conning tower, Toby could see that there were a number of uniformed men waiting for him. There was nothing he could do as they bundled him down the vertical stepladder into the bowels of the sub. No chance of arguing. Before he could reach the bottom of the steps, he'd passed out.

Toby opened his eyes to a very strange world. The walls seemed to be closing in on him; he was trapped in a large tin can.

"You've woken up!" came a familiar voice from the end of the bunk. A tousle-haired girl peered into Toby's pale face.

Tash! Thank god she's alive.

"Thought you were a goner there for a while, Tobes."

Toby tentatively felt the sore patch on his head where the plank had thwacked him. It was sticky with congealed blood. "So did I," he muttered, wincing with the throbbing in his head. "Where are we? Where are the others? Where are the Corporation taking us?"

"Oh Toby – you won't believe it," said Tash, bouncing on the bed nearer him. "We've been rescued! By the Royal Navy!"

"The Royal Navy?" Toby sat up. "You're kidding? I thought the armed forces had all collapsed years ago!"

Just then, as if to prove him wrong, there was a

knock on the door and in walked a tall, bearded man in a navy jumper with the Royal Navy insignia on the chest. The gold epaulettes on his shoulders told Toby that this was someone important.

"How's the head wound?" asked the officer.

"Er… ok I think," stuttered Toby.

"Marvellous. I'm Captain Rory McFee, in charge of this vessel. Lucky we spotted you when we did. You were headed straight for the rocks."

Toby couldn't think of anything to say – he still couldn't believe they weren't all about to be murdered by the Corporation.

"Oh, and here's someone desperate to see you," he said, smiling. Behind him, a half-drowned looking Hasif and a bedraggled Snowy scampered into the room.

Toby laughed and ruffled Snowy's damp fur. "Where's Professor MacDuff? Is she ok?"

"She'll be fine," said the captain, reassuring him. "She's in the other sick bay with our medic. Swallowed a lot of water."

"Phew!" Toby sighed. His mind turned to the vaccine, but he held his tongue.

One thing at a time; at least the Navy can help us now.

"What we need to know now is, what were you all doing in these waters?" the captain asked, turning towards Tash and Hasif. "And which commune have you come from? I didn't recognise your boat."

Toby, Tash and Hasif all started to gabble at once. Captain McFee held up his hand.

"Whoa!" he said. "One at a time – who's the eldest?"

"I'm the eldest," said Toby, taking control of the situation. "I'm not sure where to start." He rolled out of the bunk and realised that someone had dressed him in some dry, oversized tracky bottoms and a navy jumper. He went on to explain about the invasion of the Corporation and the incarceration of the islanders, including the interrogation of Dr Pettifer and the secret formulation of the vaccine. The captain furrowed and raised his eyebrows throughout the long tale.

"I rescued them from the rats and bears *and* lions!" added Hasif proudly. "I'm a warrior!"

"Umm, yes – I can see that," remarked the captain. "I can't believe you've been living alone in Edinburgh all these years. It's astounding." He turned back to question Toby, "And you say this Corporation *started* the red fever? And is now holding prisoners on Orkney?"

Why don't adults ever believe me? What do I have to do to convince him?

"Yes! But it's worse than that. Much worse!" cried Toby, wanting to shake the captain out of his air of disbelief. "We've got to get back fast to stop them experimenting on our families. Professor MacDuff has the real vaccine – or I hope she still has it. Can you help us? They have armed troops of their own."

"She won't let go of her medical box, if that's what you're referring to," said Captain McFee. "Look, I haven't got the power to just order an assault on an island simply because you claim it has been taken over by a corrupt organisation. We have no proof that the red fever was deliberately—"

"We're telling the truth!" declared Tash, standing up and clenching her fists, her face red with rage.

"Truth?" queried the captain, as if the three of them wouldn't know the truth if they fell over it. "Look, the four of you have obviously had a traumatic time. Stress can do strange things to people, especially youngsters like you. Maybe these people came to help your families?"

"Ask Professor MacDuff!" cried Toby. "She'll tell you the real truth – the Corporation was responsible for developing and spreading the red fever! They wanted full control over the vaccine so they could immunise their army and take over the world!"

"Ok, calm down," said the captain. "I've never heard of this 'Corporation', and I was informed *by the government* at the time that the red fever was a natural disaster. My job is to patrol these waters and protect St Andrews, not go on missions to save the world from evil corporations."

"St Andrews?" queried Hasif. "Why would you need to protect St Andrews?"

"That's classified information. I can't tell you," replied the captain.

Toby had a sudden flashback at the name. "I think I know!" he blurted out. "I remember seeing a map. Tash, it was in the bunker near Stirling after we'd been rescued by the Marines." "Yes, I remember," added Tash. "If it hadn't been for Snowy…" She bent down and stroked the grizzled grey head of the dog, who stared up at her with adoring eyes at the sound of his name.

"Tom – he's the commander – was quick to cover it up so I only got a glimpse. They were the sites of the other secret bunkers, weren't they?"

"Are you talking about Tom Pickett-Smyth?" said Captain McFee.

"Yes, that's him!"

"He and I were in the Special Forces together, before the red fever."

"Brilliant! You can ask him," said Toby. "He'll vouch for us."

"Ok, ok, well I can't do anything until I've spoken to my commander at base."

"Oh," sighed Toby, disconsolately. Somehow he had thought that when they'd been rescued by the Royal Navy all his troubles were over. He had pictured them sailing into battle and squashing Madame Sima and the Corporation.

Why won't they just get on with it? We can't wait for all this bureaucracy! We need to get to Orkney as soon as possible!

"Get some rest, there's nothing else you can do right now," the captain told them. "I'll let you know when I've got more information."

"What else could be more important than this?" fumed Toby, pacing the cramped chamber.

"It'll be ok," said Tash, wanting to comfort him. "Once they've spoken to Professor MacDuff and asked Tom, they'll know what a hero you've been, and then they'll believe you."

As the minutes ticked by, Toby marched impatiently up and down the small cell, infuriated by the delay in his rescue plan. Soon he could stand it no longer. He flung open the door and found himself in a narrow corridor lined with pipes and great snakes of brightly coloured cables. An overpowering smell of diesel and hot, sweaty bodies stifled the air. Although Toby was used to the pitching and rolling of the *Lucky Lady*, the strange pulsing motion of the submarine throbbing through his body made him feel queasy.

There weren't many rooms to explore in the long, thin body of the sub, and Toby quickly found the captain in the control room. Several men were staring at screens surrounded by panels of coloured lights that blinked and flashed in the dark. Captain McFee was barking orders at them as he watched small symbols chasing across the screens to the accompaniment of frenzied bleeping.

"Captain McFee? Have you got permission to sail to Orkney yet?"

The captain turned round with a start and studied Toby quizzically. His expression softened as he realised that Toby was only worried about his family.

"Well, yes and no," he replied. "Commander McPherson has decided to send drones to take pictures of Orkney in order to ascertain whether or not this Corporation exists. We need to know their exact positions and numbers. We can't just throw our forces into the unknown."

"Drones?" yelped Toby. "But that's plain stupid!"

"Oh, and you're an expert on warfare, are you?" retorted the captain crossly.

"Well I know enough to know that if the drones

are spotted, the Corporation will have time to prepare their defences. At the moment they are totally unaware that the Royal Navy still exists! Surely taking them by surprise would be a better idea?"

"Well, there is that, I suppose," said the captain. "But like I said, we have limited resources and we can't just go off on a whim."

"It's not a whim! And as for reconnaissance, Tash and I can tell you all you need to know," continued Toby. "We spent days planning how to evade them on the island. Give us a map and we'll show you where their defences are, and how best to attack."

There was a long pause while the captain considered Toby's proposal. Toby felt his stomach lurching over and over inside. So much depended on the captain agreeing with him.

"Mmm…" Captain McFee stroked his neat beard thoughtfully. "I need to run this past Commander McPherson, leave it with me."

Toby returned to the medical bay to find Tash tucking into a hot plate of baked beans, fried egg and chips. "This is so much better than rat stew, Tobes!"

But Toby was too nervous to eat. He sat on the bed, deep in his own thoughts, biting the stubs of his nails down to the quick as he waited for a decision to be made.

"Eat this, not your dirty nails," ordered Tash, shoving his plate under his nose.

Normally Toby would have given his right arm for a plate of chips but he just pushed the food around, disinterested. "Where's Hasif?"

Tash told him that Hasif had disappeared a while ago; she hadn't even noticed him leave. When he returned a few minutes later, his face was flushed with success.

"I've been sneaking round the sub." Hasif said breathlessly. "Told you I'm good at that – all those years of avoiding the gangs. You'll never guess who's hiding in that bunker in St Andrews!"

"Who?" queried Toby, not really interested.

"The royal family, the prime minister, all the important people in the military and the government!"

"Huh!" remarked Tash. "Why would they bother saving them?"

"And nearby at RAF Leuchars there's loads of the Army and Navy in hiding – jets, bombers, helicopters – the lot," continued Hasif excitedly. "They've been there all this time and we never knew!"

"That's great," said Toby sullenly, "but doesn't help us does it?"

Hasif, deflated, thumped down on the bed beside them, disappointed that his intelligence-gathering mission hadn't provoked more interest. Just then the door burst opened and in walked the captain.

"Seems like your information is correct," he stated, a smile creeping across his face.

He seems very happy about this? Maybe he's fed up with patrolling the same old dull waters round St Andrews, and fancies a bit of action!

"Commander MacPherson was very impressed that you managed to find out so much about the Corporation and their research. Seems like our special intelligence forces had their suspicions; what you've told us confirms them. There'll be no trading any vaccine today – we're going in with force to stamp this Corporation out for good."

"YES! Cried Toby.

"I've got permission for you lot to accompany us so you can advise – from a distance, of course."

"Ok, let's go NOW!" Toby didn't want to think of his dad and Sylvie in the hands of Madame Sima one second longer.

"It's not going to be a picnic, but from what Tom and Professor MacDuff have told me, you three are used to that. Right?"

"That's right!" cried Tash. "Tobes is very brave!" She reached over and hugged him.

"Er…" muttered Toby. For once he was stumped for words and stared at the floor with embarrassment as a pink flush lit his cheeks.

S'pose I've got to be brave now! Still, at last we've been taken seriously. Don't worry Dad – we're coming!

19.
DANGER IN THE NIGHT

As the cold wind bit into their bones, the three friends stood huddled in the conning tower on the deck of the lurching submarine, accompanied by a camouflaged soldier. Professor MacDuff was still safely on board the submarine with her vaccine, being questioned further about the Corporation.

A strong beam of light flared out into the dark sky, searching for the helicopter that would take them home.

"Th– this– is c-cool." stuttered Hasif, shivering. "I always wanted to be a c-commando. And now look at me!"

Toby smiled. "You look just like one, especially with all that gunk smeared over your face." He pulled the black balaclava down over his chin and tucked it into the neck of his padded stab vest.

"Now, remember to pull your night-vision goggles on after you've been dropped off," said the dark-clad soldier standing with them. "And when the chopper lands, drop down and run low – don't want you to get your heads sliced off!"

Toby wrestled his hands into his gloves. He ducked

as a passing wave swept over the side of the sub, sending spray crashing into the tower.

Thanks for that – that makes me feel so much better about the mission. That's if I don't drown first.

"Here it is!" shouted the soldier as the beam caught sight of a helicopter hovering towards them. "Who's going first?" He reached out to catch the dangling harness.

Toby could just make out a figure sitting at the open door of the chopper, controlling the wire. "I will," he announced, trying to sound braver than he felt.

"Should be able to get two of you into this," said the soldier.

"I'll go with you, Tobes," cried Tash over the noise of the crashing waves. She tossed her wild hair off her face, pulled her balaclava down and stood close to Toby so the soldier could strap them both into the harness.

"Ok!" he called, signalling to the winch man above.

Toby felt the tug of the harness around them as it started to ascend. "Hold tight!" he shouted in Tash's ear, as the wire tightened and they were pulled slowly skywards, their legs swinging helplessly beneath them.

A gust of wind snatched at their bodies as they floated through the air, pitching them sideways over the foaming sea.

Don't look down. Keep looking up. We'll be safe in a minute.

"Good fun, eh Tobes?" Tash screamed in his ear.

Toby nodded, amazed that she could be so calm when they were in danger of being ditched into the ocean, torn from the harness and drowned. He remembered all the times that Tash had come up trumps when the going got tough.

She's braver than me.

Steadily the wire inched upwards until they were level with the cabin door. The winch man leant out and pulled them roughly inside. Through the roar of the wind and the blades above him, Toby could hear a squawking babble coming from the pilot's intercom.

"What's going on?" he yelled, tugging Tash towards him.

"It's getting too windy to attempt another winch up," the man shouted over the noise. "We're going to have to leave your friend behind. Sorry."

"But we can't leave Hasif behind," cried Toby. "He'll be mad!"

"It's probably better this way Tobes," said Tash. "He's so impulsive – all that talk of being a warrior – it could get us into trouble. Besides – he can look after Snowy and Tally while we're gone."

Yeah – Tash is right. This is a mission that calls for a cool head, and it's one we might not be coming back from!

The door of the helicopter slid closed and Toby felt the great bird lift them up and away from the submarine.

The soldier opposite handed them headphones for keeping in contact with Captain McFee over the snarling rumble of the engines, and signalled for them to make themselves comfortable in the cramped cabin. The two friends curled up together and settled down for the long trip. Toby was soon aware of the soft rise and fall of Tash's breath as the helicopter motion sent her to sleep, but every time he closed his eyes all he could see was Madame Sima looming over Sylvie, a large needle in her hand.

Poor Sylvie, she must think I've abandoned her. I wonder how Jamie is, and Katie and the Pettifers... I hope Dad hasn't lost faith in me.

As he lay there, going over and over the worst scenarios in his head, he became aware of the noise of more engines reverberating through the night.

Must be a whole battalion of helicopters – I hope the Corporation doesn't blast us out of the sky when they hear us coming.

Eventually his eyelids drooped and he fell into a fitful sleep, peopled with soldiers in blood-red uniforms marching endlessly across Scotland, Madame Sima at their head.

"Toby! Wake up! We're here."

He opened his eyes to see Tash crouched over him, her night-vision goggles pulled down, making her look like a robotic owl. A blast of freezing air gusted over him, bringing him sharply to his senses. He could hear the pilot counting down to landing, telling them to be ready to jump. He grabbed his rucksack, pulled down his goggles, and sat waiting for the order to go.

The door slid open and a black-clad figure leaned in. A familiar voice shouted in his ear.

"Hello Toby! Fancy meeting you here." It was Tom Pickett-Smyth, the commander from the Stirling bunker. He reached forward and helped Toby jump down. "And Natasha! Quick! Hop down!"

They landed lightly on their feet and started to run, heads bent low, out into the dark. Around them a dozen or so helicopters were discharging their cargo of soldiers.

"This way," cried Tom as he motioned towards a copse of woodland. Toby grabbed hold of Tash's hand and they ran for cover. The helicopters disappeared as quickly as they had arrived, swooping over the headland and back out to sea.

"They're not leaving us, are they?" Toby asked Tom as they stopped to catch their breath.

"No, they're going to wait on Burray until we give the signal for the attack," he replied, "then they'll give us air cover. The aim is to destroy the enemy's choppers before they've a chance to get them off the ground. We're assuming they don't have any land-to-air missiles."

Toby gulped.

Glad I didn't know that before – I might not have got on that helicopter. If this plan doesn't work we could all be stuck on this island at the mercy of Madame Sima.

"Good to be back in action, eh Toby?" Tom slapped him on his back and grinned. "Ok, let's have a look…"

Tom spread a map at his feet, a small torch in his hand.

"We're here – southeast of the fort," he said, pointing to the map. "According to the information you gave Captain McFee, there are troops here and here, some at Kirkwall, and their choppers are parked here."

"Yep," said Toby and Tash in unison, craning their necks to peer at the map.

"The fort walls are three metres high," commented Tash. "My dad built them good and strong. And inside there is an inner ditch full of spiked posts. He got the idea from Fort George. Didn't help against the Corporation though."

"Ok," said Tom "Don't worry about the fort – my commandos will breach the walls and storm the inner buildings. Once we've made the area safe I'll take you in and you can lead us to the prisoners. You must check to see if everyone is accounted for. Don't worry – me and my men will be right beside you."

Worry? Huh! What is there to worry about? Only a fort full of well-armed troopers!

"We know where the islanders will be," said Tash, "but George and Layla Pettifer were being held in a separate building when we left."

"One thing at a time. Come with me!" cried Tom folding his map and signalling to his troops to move forward. Keeping tight beside Tom, Toby and Tash moved stealthily through the undergrowth. They were soon out the other side of the trees and skirting around open fields, keeping close to the straggling wind-scarred hedges. Before long Toby could make out the lights of the fort twinkling in the distance.

Not far now. Hold on Dad – we're coming.

As they approached the walls, Tom motioned for Toby and Tash to stop behind an old stone bothy. "Stay here, just a second, whilst I give the order to attack. Don't budge, I'll be right back!"

Toby and Tash nestled into the walls, peering round the corner to watch the commandos throwing grappling hooks at the walls and scuttling up them like black spiders.

"They're ace, these goggles, aren't they?" whispered Tash.

"Yeah," muttered Toby. "But why do we have to stay here? I want to be up front – I just know that Sima will try to slip away rather than fight. How are they going to know where everybody is?" He peered round the wall, and saw Tom ordering the assault with his back to them. "We can give Tom the slip if we run now."

"You're mad! We've got to wait until Madame Sima and her troops are captured. You don't want to get shot, do you? We're to stay here. That was the plan."

"Yeah, well, I've got a better plan," said Toby, wriggling round the side of the bothy.

"What? Are you crazy? How are we going to get into the fort?" exclaimed Tash.

"The same way we got out, silly. Through the hole in the wire by Snowy's kennel, then the pipes. Coming?" Keeping a low profile, Toby trotted off towards the far side of the fort, skirting round the Corporation's watchtowers.

Tash, shaking her head in disbelief, followed.

With his night goggles on, Toby could see the perimeter track around the fort clearly. He soon arrived at a large hollow that they had dug in the soft sandy soil to escape just a few days previously.

"Here!" he hissed at Tash. "You go first."

Tash squirmed under the fence and Toby quickly

wriggled after her. Just as they stood up in the brightly lit inner yard, it was plunged into darkness.

"That must've been the commandos," remarked Tash.

"We'd better stay out of their way," warned Toby, watching the shadowy figures of the commandos creeping round towards the main entrance. They stopped under the windows and Toby saw them smash the glass and lob something inside.

Ear-splitting explosions shattered the peaceful night as they felt the blast right across the yard. Immediately chaos ensued: a siren went off, someone inside started shouting orders, the distinctive rattle of gunfire began, and the commandos slunk into the building.

"Quick!" Toby shouted. "We need to get inside and find Sima before she escapes or takes hostages!"

Together they sprinted towards Madame Sima's interrogation room. Edging cautiously up to the window, Toby peered inside, half expecting to see his Dad and Sylvie in chains.

The room was empty.

Where are they? Where's Madame Sima?

Tash was busy pulling the heavy grid away from the entrance to the drains they had escaped through. "Huh," she panted. "Give us a hand."

Toby helped her wrestle the grating to the ground, then they scrambled down into the dank darkness.

"Can you remember which way?" asked Toby nervously. This had seemed such a good idea, but now they were faced with the labyrinth of twists and turns in the blackness, he couldn't decide which way to go.

"Follow me," she said confidently. "I have very good sense of direction. We need to go left here…"

Toby caught hold of her hand and, holding tight, stumbled after her as she nimbly skipped along the low passageway.

"Here it is; this is where we came down from the loos," she said, stopping under the large concrete slab they had moved to cover their tracks. The two of them clambered up the mound of stones they'd left in their wake, and sliding the slab sideways, climbed out.

"Right – we've got to try and get to the hall without being seen," said Toby. "Just hope nobody notices us in the confusion."

Swirls of violent green smoke from the stun grenades curled down the corridor as Toby and Tash sneaked their way to the hall. As they got nearer they could hear soldiers shouting, children screaming, and Murdo, another elder of the commune, calling for calm.

What met their eyes as they entered the hall was anything but calm. The frightened islanders were huddled against the back wall of the isolation chamber, clasping cloths to their mouths and noses. Corporation troopers charged past them in a blind panic, not noticing Toby and Tash creeping through the murky cloud towards the tall mesh gates that imprisoned their families and friends.

"The blast has damaged the lock," Toby mouthed to Tash as he rattled the mangled grid door. "If we hit it together we might be able to open it."

The two of them took a step back then flung themselves at the gate. It buckled and twisted then gave way under their weight and they fell into the pen.

Toby picked himself up and searched frantically for his dad and Sylvie amongst the crowd of petrified faces.

"Toby, Natasha! Never thought I'd see you two again!" yelled Murdo, coughing and spluttering into a wet rag.

"Come with us!" cried Toby. "We know a way out – keep everyone together."

"Where?" shouted Murdo, as a loud burst of sporadic gunfire sounded off nearby. Tash was hurriedly rounding up the prisoners and ushering them towards the door.

"Where are Dad and Sylvie?" yelled Toby. "And Katie and Jamie? Why aren't they here with you?"

Murdo shook his head as he shepherded a couple of young mothers, clutching their infants, out of the gate. "The guards took them away," he told Toby. "I don't know where they've taken them."

"What?" cried Toby. He didn't care about finding Sima now; he just wanted his family to be safe.

They could be anywhere on the island. Think, Toby! Think!

20.
A RISKY RESCUE

"Let's get everyone out of here first," said Tash, who had found her mum and dad and was hugging them tightly, tears cascading down her face. "I'll take them to the tunnel, then come back and help you find your family."

Toby raced back towards the loos and slithered down into the hole.

They must be here somewhere – unless they've taken them off the island? Think! Where would Madame Sima hold them? ... Wait – I know!

Stumbling his way along the sewer he came to the opening near the lab. He scrambled back up and out into the dark yard and hesitated, searching for signs of the troopers. They seemed to have all retreated into the main building. Taking no risks, Toby darted around the outhouses that circled the main courtyard until he came to a low row of pens that used to house Snowy – and Belle.

"Belle!" he shouted. "Belle!"

She will find Katie and Jamie – she'll sniff her owners out!

An excited bark issued from behind one of the doors. Toby frantically opened the door with shaking hands and out jumped a great white furry bundle, wagging her tail and wriggling with delight.

"Oh Belle! Am I glad to see you!" said Toby, wrapping his arms around her, avoiding her slobbery wet tongue as it attempted to wash his face. "Go and find your mum! Go find!" he ordered, pushing her away from him. Belle danced around him first, then, sniffing the air, set off at a gallop towards the far end of the fort.

Toby ran to keep up with her, but he was thrown off balance as the ground shook with a deep rumble and the night sky was illuminated with a flash. A series of brilliant explosions mushroomed into fiery clouds in the distance.

The Commandos must be blowing up the Corporation's helicopters. Either that, or Sima's troops are fighting back!

More gunfire could be heard coming from the main hall, along with shouts and screams. The Corporation troops seemed to be putting up a real fight.

Hurry up Toby! If the commandos lose this battle, we're in deep trouble!

Toby called out to Belle again and heard a muffled woof coming from round the back of the furthest cabin. Following the noise, he found her whining and jumping up at a door that was securely fastened with a large padlock and chain.

"Dad? You in there?" cried Toby. "Katie?"

"Toby!?" cried a familiar voice.

"Dad! The Navy are here to rescue you but we need to get out of the fort quick. Looks like Sima's troops are putting up a fight. Stand back – I'll smash the lock." He glanced around for a rock or plank he could sever the chain with, then remembered that he still had a crowbar in his rucksack from when they'd escaped. He rummaged in his bag and pulled out the cold metal tool. With it firmly gripped in his hands, he tried to lever the chain from the door.

"It won't budge!" shouted Toby, as he grunted and groaned, throwing all his weight behind it.

"Try the handle, Toby," called Katie from the other side. Toby hitched the bar through the metal handle and tried again, then again and again. Just as he was about to give up, a huge tearing sound rendered the air, and the handle ripped from the door, taking the lock with it.

"YES!" cried Toby, as out of the open door tumbled his dad, carrying a sleepy Sylvie, and trailed by a hollow-eyed Katie who grabbed Belle and looked frantically around her.

Toby threw down the crowbar and raced to hug his dad and little sister.

"Toby?" mumbled Sylvie, pushing her blonde hair out of her eyes. "I told Daddy you'd come and rescue us."

"Toby – thank god you're alright – what a fright you gave us disappearing like that," said his dad. He looked drawn and exhausted, his thin face telling the horror of what they'd been through.

"Toby! Where's Jamie?" gushed Katie, squeezing his shoulder tightly. "Where is Jamie?"

Toby's heart stopped. "Isn't he with you?"

"No, you all disappeared together," replied Katie. "Toby?"

Behind Katie, a very thin and dishevelled Layla Pettifer stumbled out, supported by a weary George Pettifer.

Toby didn't want to think about what might have happened to Jamie. He couldn't look Katie in the eye. "I'll explain in a bit – we've got to get out of the fort quickly. Follow me."

How am I going to explain to Jamie's mum that we left him alone on the island when we took off on Lucky Lady? *What if the guards caught him?*

"Where are you taking us?" asked Toby's dad, as the five of them cautiously edged their way round the perimeter of the yard, Belle bouncing at their heels.

"We have to go down here," said Toby, as they crept back to the drains. "It's going to be ok, Sylvie, don't worry," he tried to sound reassuring as his sister clung tightly onto him.

"I was SO scared Tobes. That horrible woman came and took us away. And I've lost Henry!" She burst into tears and rubbed her grimy face on his jacket. "Poor Henry! He'll be so frightened without me."

"I'll find him, but we need to get to safety just now," soothed Toby, passing her back to his dad.

Katie's eyes were still searching his when she helped Professor Pettifer, who was shaking and shivering, down into the hole.

"These drains pass under the fort wall and come up in the middle of Heathery Howes. It's not far then to that bothy the other side of Hamly Hill. The Navy landed over that way. You should be safe there, for a while anyway."

"Well done, Toby. I'm so proud of you," said his dad, clasping Toby's arm and shaking it.

Yeah, well we're not out of the storm yet Dad, let's leave the congratulations until Madame Sima's under lock and key and Jamie's safe too.

Toby turned back to struggle out of the drains.

"Where are you going?" asked his dad, anxiously.

"To get Jamie," replied Toby, over his shoulder. "Don't worry I'll take Belle with me – she'll sniff him out."

"Toby, come back!" ordered his dad, but Toby wasn't listening. He was already retracing his steps, Belle quietly at his side as she sensed the urgency of his movements.

A flare screeched up into the sky, bursting into violent pink shards of light that lit the square with an unearthly aura. Toby glanced across to see more Navy soldiers creeping through the shadows towards the main building. Short, staccato bursts of gunfire reverberated through the night air as they fought their way in. Then another explosion rocked the foundations of the fort. Dust and debris spewed into the air to hang in an ominous cloud over the battle.

"Come on Belle," hissed Toby through clenched teeth. "I think I know where Jamie might be!"

21.
SLIPPERY SIMA

Ignoring the constant barrage of mayhem behind him, Toby squeezed under the fence, adjusted his night-vision goggles and set off at a jog across the fields. Belle trotted obediently at his heels. On the brow of a hill he stopped to catch his breath and study the scene of conflict he'd left behind. It was impossible to say who was winning. A heavy haze of thick smoke swirled over the fort, and he could still hear angry shouting and sporadic volleys erupting.

Ok Toby, concentrate on finding Jamie. Dad can organise the others; he's in charge now.

As he approached the town of Kirkwall, which lay nestled against the coastline, Toby slowed his pace. He could hear a vehicle roaring towards him, and saw its bright headlights sweeping the road. Toby grabbed Belle and pulled her into a narrow ginnel, pressing himself back into the shadows.

A truck full of animated soldiers flashed past. He could hear their frenzied yells over the growl of the engine.

Corporation guards! Good – that means there'll be none patrolling the town.

Keeping a watchful eye open, slipping in and out of the doorways, he made his way to the centre of the town. Here the majestic Earl's Palace lay in ruins opposite St Magnus Cathedral. With Belle sniffing the way, Toby leapt over the fragments of broken stone and disappeared through what had once been a palatial entrance garlanded with tiers of ornate carvings. Now, the harsh winters of Orkney had taken their toll and eroded the soft stone to a leave just a semblance of the grandeur it once had.

"Jamie?" Toby called out. He was sure that his friend would be here somewhere. Jamie had always loved to explore the ancient ruins with their high vaulted windows and the labyrinth of deep cellars. It would be an ideal place to hide, and Belle seemed to have caught a scent.

"Go on Belle, find Jamie!" encouraged Toby, pushing the big white dog forwards. Belle looked around and sniffed the air, then the ground. With one yelp she shot away into the dark depths of the cloisters that ran round the palace's L-shaped carcass.

Belle's bark grew fainter. Toby followed the noise, pattering down a flight of steps and into the bowels of the building. The cellars were dank and smelt of old bones and bodies; Toby remembered some of the murky stories Jamie had told them about the poor people of Orkney who had suffered there. He shivered.

Get a grip! There's nothing here more frightening than Madame Sima.

He stopped and listened for the scratchy padding of Belle's paws on stone.

Nothing.

The hairs on the back of Toby's neck stood on end as an icy splinter of fear slithered down his spine.

"Got you!" yelled a voice in his ear as something reached out and grabbed his shoulders.

Toby jumped into the air. "Jamie! Don't do that!"

"How did you know where to find me?" asked Jamie, shaking his long, fair hair from his eyes. "I've been hiding in the cathedral; it's warmer there, but when I heard the commotion kick off, thought I'd be safer down here. What's happening? Is everyone ok?"

"Yes, your mum and everyone are out safe. Come on," said Toby, making his way back up the steps. "We've got to get down to the harbour and see if there are enough boats to get everyone off the island in case the Navy don't win. Then we've got to…"

"Whoa, slow down, you brought the Navy?" said Jamie.

"I'll explain as we go," said Toby.

Jamie showed Toby out of the ruins while Belle bounded around them. "You did a lot in a few days – I'm amazed you got back so quickly," enthused Jamie. "Did you find MacDuff?"

"Yeah we did, but it wasn't what we expected…" Toby filled in Jamie with the bare details of the journey to Edinburgh, meeting the boy-warrior Hasif, finding the professor and finally being rescued by the Royal Navy. He left out the part where they discovered that MacDuff and the Pettifers had developed the virus for the Corporation; that could come later.

"Wow!" cried Jamie. "That's not fair. I've just spent

the whole time sneaking around Kirkwall worrying about you all. Got into the supply barn that your dad and Murdo set up at the docks, so I didn't go hungry. But I had to be careful; the place was crawling with Corporation troops."

The two boys and the dog had reached the small stone-built harbour, which was no longer bathed in the glare of security lights. A flotilla of small boats bobbed where they were moored in the choppy waters.

"Woof!" said Belle, turning to stand facing the town, her hackles raised.

"What's the matter Belle?" Jamie asked uneasily.

"Hide!" exclaimed Toby as another large black Jeep came careering down the icy street towards them. They ducked down behind an upturned boat that had been left on the quayside just as the truck slewed to a halt.

The front doors were flung open. Two darkly-clad figures jumped out and hauled some large bags out from the boot.

"It's Madame Sima!" hissed Toby, peering over the boat. "And a bodyguard."

"What are we going to do?" whispered Jamie. "She's escaping!"

"Over my dead body," growled Toby. "I'm going to stop her."

"Toby! She's armed and extremely dangerous!" gasped Jamie, clinging onto Toby's arm. "Leave it to the Navy – they'll get her."

"It's too late for that. She's probably got a sub lying off the coast to take her back to their base," said Toby, trying to keep the tremble from his voice. "She's not going to get away with everything she's done."

He took a peek out and saw Madame Sima and her bodyguard loading the bags onto an inflatable rib moored to the side of the quay. Toby slipped out of his jacket and took off his boots.

"What are you doing?" asked an incredulous Jamie.

"Wait here," instructed Toby, inching towards the harbour wall. He kept low until he reached a flight of steps reaching down into the dark waters of the harbour. Bracing himself for the cold, he lowered himself gingerly into the sea.

The freezing chill hit him like a brick wall, forcing the air from his lungs as he gasped with the pain of what felt like a thousand sharp needles piercing his chest.

Where's that chain Dad used to tie up the Lucky Lady? *It's anchored to a bollard – if I can just get the hook on the other end...*

He quietly struck out into the water, teeth chattering, keeping as close to the harbour wall as possible until he had reached *Lady's* former spot. Hanging down under the surface dangled the chunky chain, its other end securely fastened on the quayside. Toby grabbed hold of it and paddled quietly out towards the rib. It was difficult swimming with the heavy chain in his hand but Toby kept going, using his free hand pull him through the excruciatingly cold water. He bumped up against the rubber side of the inflatable and snatched at the outboard motor to steady himself. Then he passed the chain around the bulk of the motor and secured the hook back onto the chain in a loop.

There! That should do it! They won't be going very far – maybe if we can slow them down, help will arrive soon.

"Is that everything?" An imperious voice rang out in the frosty air. "Hurry up, man! The Interceptor is rendezvousing with us in one hour precisely."

Toby's heart hammered in his frozen chest; Madame Sima and her thug were descending the steps down to the boat, carrying even more bags. He was just a few feet from them. One false move and he and his plan would be exposed.

Don't move! Don't cough!

He filled his lungs with air in one gigantic breath and then pushed away from the boat, letting himself slip under the surface, going down, down, down. He could feel his fingers and toes going numb and hard as ice. As the blackness enveloped him, he could hear the babble of voices reverberating through the murk above. When he had sunk far enough he kicked out with his legs sideways and silently glided back to the harbour wall, surfacing some way from the rib, which now had its two passengers safely on board. They were too busy packing the bags and looking at maps to notice the dripping figure slinking surreptitiously from the sea.

"Toby, what did you do? I couldn't see in the dark," asked Jamie, wrapping Toby in his coat as he appeared from behind the wall.

"W...W...Wait and see..." stammered Toby, his teeth chattering non-stop. He pulled Jamie's thick jacket round himself and slid down onto the ground.

The sound of an engine roared out from the quayside as Madame Sima and her guard prepared to leave. Their boat swung away from the quayside, picking up speed as it headed out towards the open seas.

NO! I thought the chain would stop them! What's happened?

But just as Toby's heart sank with the thought of the failure of his plan, the boat reached the end of the chain and jerked to a violent halt, throwing the bow up into the air. Screams rendered the night as the two occupants were thrown into the churning water, to thrash wildly about as the boat's engine whined and whizzed in the air. The boat thumped back down to one side of them, and then veered to the right, motor still running, and hit the wooden pier at speed.

A huge orange and black fireball soared into the sky as the fuel-filled boat exploded, throwing fragments of wreckage around the harbour for hundreds of metres. For one moment Toby considered leaving them in the freezing water, but the thought of justice spurred him into action.

With a ringing in his ears from the explosion, Toby leapt up and ran for a lifebuoy hanging on a post by the quay.

"Help me!" he shouted to Jamie. "Can't let her drown – that would be too good for her."

Jamie ran to another lifebuoy and tugged it down from its stand.

"I'll throw them," commanded Toby, grinning at Jamie. "Got bigger pecs than you!" He stepped back and took aim at the struggling survivors surrounded by the debris from the boat, threw one buoy and then the other.

Toby and Jamie waited until Madame Sima had grabbed hold of a buoy, then started to pull her in, using the long rope attached.

As she neared the steps, Toby called out, "You going to behave yourself?" He let the rope fall slack. "Shout up – we can't hear you! We're not going to rescue you unless you promise."

"YES!" yelled the half-drowned figure, crazily splashing about in the harbour below them.

"Ok," Toby laughed. He had lost his terror of Madame Sima; she seemed pathetic now, robbed of all her finery and without the support of her troops.

As they dragged her to the bottom of the harbour steps, Madame Sima pulled herself out of the water, sobs heaving in her chest as she shook and shivered in a pool of icy water.

"Tie her up," commanded Toby.

Jamie grabbed her wrists, pulled them behind her back and tied them up tightly with an old rope attached to a bollard. He wasn't going to take any chances.

Toby went to pick up the rope from the other lifebuoy when he noticed that the soldier was striking out for the other side of the harbour. Kicking furiously with his feet, he was propelling himself on the buoy out of their reach.

"Don't worry about him," said Jamie. "He doesn't look like he's interested in Madame Sima any more."

Madame Sima winced and turned away.

Toby turned to talk to Jamie, but suddenly his legs turned to jelly and he abruptly sat down on a bollard.

"You ok, Tobes?" asked Jamie.

"Just feel a bit… wobbly, that's all." The flickering flames from the wrecked boat danced in front of his eyes, and his head felt very heavy. Too heavy. He doubled over and took several deep breaths.

"You're probably in shock," said Jamie. "I'm not surprised! That water is freezing. You did an amazing thing with that chain."

"Yeah – I saw it in a movie a long time ago. Now we've just got to get her back to the fort."

"Woof!" barked Belle as if in agreement. Then she carried on barking.

"What's up Belle?" said Jamie, trying to calm her, but the dog was now bouncing off all fours, staring into the sky.

"A chopper's coming," observed Jamie, pointing to a speck of light that was approaching from further inland.

"We'd better hide," gasped Toby, staggering to his feet. "Let's get her over to that fisherman's shed. It could be more of her guards…"

"Ok," agreed Jamie, hastily undoing the knot from the bollard.

Together they dragged Sima, shouting and screaming, over to the shed. Inside was a stack of cobwebbed lobster pots, and on the walls were draped some dusty old fishing nets. Toby rubbed the grimy glass of the small window with his cuff as the two pools of light from the helicopter got nearer and nearer.

190

"Is it… them?" gulped Jamie. "We'd better gag her or else they'll hear."

Toby squinted up as the huge metal bird hovered overhead and slowly came to rest on the strip of tarmac at the harbour front.

"I don't think we need to do that!" he exclaimed. "Look – there's no Corporation logo on the side. It's the Royal Navy! They've come for us!"

Leaving the moaning Madame Sima in the shed, the two boys ran out laughing and crying as the helicopter's engine died and its blades stopped whizzing. The door slid open and out jumped Tash and…

"DAD!" shrieked Toby dashing up and flinging himself into his dad's outstretched arms. "Am I glad to see you!"

"Where's my mum?" asked a tearful Jamie.

"She's back at the fort with Sylvie and the others. She'll be so glad you're safe. *Everyone's* safe, thanks to you kids. Looks like Sima got away, but the rest of her thugs are under arrest and…"

"No, she's hasn't!" yelled Toby, pointing to the shed. "She's in there."

22.
THE JOURNEY'S END

As the warm spring sunshine filtered through the windows of the dormitory, Toby lifted his sleepy head from his pillow and contemplated the day ahead. His dad had promised a picnic on the beach to celebrate Sylvie's birthday and she had been getting very excited about it.

Toby sprang out of bed and went to rouse Jamie, who was still fast asleep in the bed opposite.

"Come on, you bedbug! Let's go and help get the picnic ready," Toby laughed and pulled back the covers.

"I'm coming," mumbled Jamie, his blond hair tumbled over his face.

In the big hall there remained no sign of the violent battle that had been fought between the Corporation's troops and the Navy. Gone was the plastic sheeting, the wire fencing and metal doors. Instead the hall was festooned with balloons, bunting and fairy lights that Toby, Tash and Jamie had helped to decorate the night before. The walls were decked with banners saying, 'Happy birthday Sylvie!', and pictures the children had painted of cakes and candles. Toby had hung up one special picture that he had rescued with

Tash: the one of a clown that Sylvie had scribbled back at the lighthouse.

"Your dad and Katie have already gone down to the beach," called Tash, running into the hall followed by Snowy. "Have you got Sylvie's present?"

"Yep," Toby said, holding up the Sylvanian rabbit family he took from the House of Hasif. "What about you?"

"It's a secret!" Tash smiled and tapped her nose conspiratorially. "Wait and see."

The three friends went round to the kennels to find Belle and her puppies.

"Wow! They're getting huge!" cried Toby as the bundles of white fur spilled out of the kennel and bounced over to him. "I'm going ask Dad if we can have one. I still miss Monty."

"You'll be lucky," grinned Jamie, as the dogs jumped all over him, smothering him with sloppy kisses. "Get down!" He laughed and tried to push away the exuberant pups.

"Where's Hasif got to?" asked Tash, pulling Snowy's tail out of a puppy's mouth. Snowy stood with a dignified look on his face, but actually seemed to be enjoying all the attention.

"He was up early to go and play football with the other kids. He's obsessed with it." remarked Toby as they started to walk from the fort.

"No wonder, bet he's loving playing with all his new mates," said Jamie. "Don't think I could have survived that long on my own."

"No, you're a right wimp," teased Toby.

"No, Tobes, if it hadn't been for Jamie, we'd have never got away from the island," said Tash, putting her arm around Jamie.

Funny, I never thought these two would become such good friends.

Outside the fort walls the three friends stopped to watch Hasif and his pals kicking a football across a muddy patch of grass. Here, the scars of the invasion still remained, with deep tracks carved out of the field where the Corporation's troops had abandoned their vehicles.

"Hiya!" yelled Hasif, running up when he saw them. "Are you going down to the beach?"

"Yep," said Toby.

"I'll just go and fetch Tally," said Hasif. "Can I bring Jenny and Lily?"

"Yeah, the party is for everyone," Toby told him.

As they walked over the headland, they could see several Navy warships anchored out in the bay. The blue-grey boats were a reminder to everyone that the island was now at peace; the threat of the Corporation was at an end. The Army had rounded up the last of Sima's troops and the Navy had taken possession of the Interceptor, the Corporation's submarine that Madame Sima had tried so desperately to reach.

As Tash stopped to pick the first of the spring flowers that nodded in the breeze, Toby watched the dogs frolicking down the sandy path to the beach.

"Hi Dad!" he yelled as they reached the sheltered sandy cove.

"Give us a hand with this gazebo," called his dad. "Then I can get the barbeque going."

Toby rushed to help his dad put up the white gazebo while Katie busied herself piling cupcakes, éclairs and scones onto pretty patterned crockery. Jamie and Tash pulled out colourful bunting from a box and draped it around on sticks.

"It looks really pretty. Sylvie will love it!" Tash declared.

"I'll go get her now," said Toby's dad, as the rest of them put out tables and deckchairs. "Won't be long."

As Toby's dad wound his way back up the path, the rest of the islanders arrived. Hasif led the way, clutching Tally, and surrounded by giggling girls. Toby smiled to himself as he stacked sandwiches onto a platter.

Hasif's certainly very popular! I knew he would love it here.

As everyone gathered round, two figures in uniform appeared on the hill.

"Look, it's Tom!" cried Toby. "But who's that with him?"

As the figures approached, Toby realised that Tom's companion was none other than Captain Rory McFee, from the sub that had rescued him and the others from the sea.

"Hi, Toby, Tash, and Hasif. This must be your friend and fellow adventurer, Jamie," said the captain, shaking their hands in turn.

"So pleased to see you," enthused Toby, "but what are you doing here?"

But before the captain could answer, the Pettifers and Professor Shona MacDuff had come to chat to the two soldiers.

Tash sidled up to Toby. "Look, Layla Pettifer is actually talking now."

"Yeah, Katie told me that she's been so much better since Shona got here. They've had time to talk it all through, come to terms with everything that happened. I'm not sure they'll ever stop feeling guilty, but she's improving every day."

"What you two whispering about?" Jamie had snuck up on them.

"Ooh, Jamie. What are you giving Sylvie?" asked Tash.

"It's a secret." Jamie smiled and winked.

Just then an old, battered Land Rover crested the hill.

"Here she comes!" shouted Murdo. "Get ready!"

Everyone hid inside the gazebo and held their breath as the truck grew near. When it came to a stop, they could hear Toby's dad talking to Sylvie. He got out of the car and led her towards them.

"Count down from five, then you can take off your blindfold."

The blindfolded Sylvie was dressed in a silver tutu and pink sequinned cardigan. As she pulled the cloth from her eyes, everyone shouted:

"HAPPY BIRTHDAY SYLVIE!"

Toby wished he had brought his camera to catch the wondrous look of surprise on his little sister's face.

"OH!" was all Sylvie could manage before she broke into a huge grin and rushed up to hug everyone in turn.

After she had blown out the candles on her huge carrot cake and everyone had sung 'Happy Birthday', it was time to open the presents. The islanders had given her a white pom-pom hat, a bag of fudge, a smart red leather satchel, and a pair of velveteen slippers. Her dad had managed to find and restore a small bike that he had painted bright blue and attached a basket to. He'd even knitted a cover for the seat and tied ribbons to the handlebars.

"Here," said Toby, handing over his parcel, lovingly wrapped in paper he had decorated with rabbits.

Sylvie tore it open and gasped with amazement when she saw the cute Sylvanian rabbit family.

"I love them, Tobes!" she shrieked, but then her face fell flat, and her nose wrinkled up as she came close to tears. "Oh, it reminds me of Henry – I miss him so much."

"Here," said Tash, coming forward with a basket. "Maybe this will help." Sylvie tentatively opened the lid and peered inside.

"Henry!" she cried, pulling out the soft brown bunny. "Where did you find him?"

"Well, it wasn't easy," said Tash. "He'd been hiding with the wild rabbits in the clover field. Actually it was Snowy that found him."

"Oh, thank you, thank you," sobbed Sylvie.

"And here is our present," declared Jamie, stepping from behind a table. "This is Beau, one of Belle's puppies – well, he's not really a puppy any more, but he is yours."

"Really?" squealed Sylvie. "Is that ok, Dad?"

"Yes, Katie asked me first and I agreed, though I think you should share him with Toby – he'll grow to be such a big dog, it'll take two of you to look after him." He grinned at Katie, who leant over and kissed him.

"Wow! Thanks Jamie, thanks Katie," said Toby, grinning from ear to ear. "He's lovely."

"I didn't have anything to give you," said Hasif, appearing next to Sylvie. "But your dad has promised we can visit Edinburgh when things go back to the way they were, so my present will be a ride in my bestest car – probably my Aston Martin."

"Yes, yes Hasif. We'll have to see about that," said Toby's dad. "The police might not be too keen on under-age drivers once law and order is restored" He laughed and ruffled Hasif's hair.

"Seeing as everyone is here, and it's a special occasion, we wanted to do something else to recognise what certain people here have done for our community," continued Toby's dad. "We are very lucky to have two of our heroes here today; Captain Rory McFee and Major Tom Pickett-Smyth. Please welcome them."

When the clapping had died down, Tom cleared his throat and addressed the islanders.

"As you all know, we as a human race have come through a terrible ordeal: the last few years have not been easy for any of us. But things are about to change. You'll be pleased to hear that what's left of government is being restored, their first priority being to produce bulk loads of freely available vaccinations. This means that the whole world will soon be immunised. Also, measures are under way to set up communications between communities like this; you are not alone any more."

At this point Captain McFee stood forward and spoke.

"Their second priority is to provide communities with the means to produce food and safe drinking water. We've just brought you a set of new generators and some industrial-sized wind turbines," he told them. "These will enable you to set up greenhouses, grow fruit and vegetables, and build a full-sized dairy."

The islanders began to clap and cheer. Tom raised his hand for silence and spoke again. "But what the Captain and I are really here to tell you is that the government has decided to honour certain people here who have put their lives in danger, have battled against a brutal regime, and have gone far beyond the call of duty in their fight for the survival of mankind. Ladies and gentlemen, I would like to ask you to give a round of applause for our heroes, Tash Gablinski, Jamie McTavish, Hasif Patel, and Toby Tennant."

Tom pulled out of his jacket pocket a box in which lay four gold medals. As the crowd cheered he placed one round the necks of each of the four proud friends.

"Speech!" someone shouted.

"Go on Tobes, say something," whispered Tash.

"Yeah, say something," said Jamie.

"Yeah, warrior!" chipped in Hasif.

Toby looked around and saw the smiling faces of his friends and family around him, Words could not describe the great welling of happiness that threatened to burst from his heart.

So he just grinned.

THE END